DATE DUE

APR 2 7 1993	SEP 1 4 2000
AUG 1 8 1993	
SEP 4 - 1993	JUL 0 9 2002
FEB 5 1994	SEP 0 7 2006
MAY 2 1 1994	OCT 1 2 2006
JUL 2 0 1994	
OCT 2 4 1994	JUL 1 8 2007
AUG 2 8 1996	MAR 2 9 2008
NOV 1 3 1996	
MAR 3 0 19	
MAY 31	
FEB 2 1 2006	

D1112871

1

AN OBSCURE GRAVE

SARA WOODS
AN OBSCURE GRAVE

'A little, little grave, an obscure grave.'
Richard II, Act II, scene iii

St. Martin's Press
New York

Library of Congress Cataloging in Publication Data

Woods, Sara, pseud.
  An obscure grave.

  I. Title.
PR6073.06303   1985   823'.914   84-23737
ISBN 0-312-58053-3

First published in Great Britain by Macmillan London Ltd.

First U.S. Edition

10 9 8 7 6 5 4 3 2 1

Any work of fiction whose characters were of uniform excellence could rightly be condemned – by that fact if by no other – as being incredibly dull. Therefore no excuse can be considered necessary for the villainy or folly of the people appearing in this book. It seems extremely unlikely that any one of them should resemble a real person, alive or dead. Any such resemblance is completely unintentional and without malice.

S.W.

Trinity Term, 1975

Tuesday, 15th July

'I have a young friend in Chedcombe,' said Vera, Lady Harding, abruptly, taking advantage of a small silence that had developed. Her nephew by marriage, Antony Maitland (whose worst enemies had never doubted his intelligence, though his uncle, Sir Nicholas Harding, had been known to do so at considerable length) gave her a look almost equally compounded of amusement and suspicion.

'I'm sure you've many friends there of all ages,' he agreed. 'But what's so special about this one?'

'She's a solicitor,' said Vera. 'Nice girl,' she added, reverting to her more usual elliptical mode of speech. 'Should have said she practises in Chedcombe, because actually she lives in Madingley, about five miles away.'

It was Tuesday evening, and, as was customary, the Hardings were dining with Antony and his wife, Jenny. This involved no more exertion than walking up two flights of stairs, because the Maitlands had occupied for many years now the two top floors of Sir Nicholas Harding's house in Kempenfeldt Square. It was a long time since anyone had referred to the arrangement as a temporary one, and over the years certain pleasant customs had grown up, with none of which Sir Nicholas's marriage four years previously to Miss Vera Langhorne, barrister-at-law, had interfered in the slightest. Originally Sir Nicholas had thrown himself on Jenny's mercy more or less as a refugee, his housekeeper, Mrs Stokes, being a lady well set in her ways among which was a visit to the cinema every Tuesday evening. So here they all were, drinking their sherry and talking in a desultory way about the day's affairs. Jenny had long been accustomed to legal shop, as her husband was in his uncle's chambers, and she and Antony wondered sometimes whether Vera hadn't some slight regret for her own practice on the West Midland circuit. However, that wasn't the point at issue now.

'The first time we met, Vera,' Antony reminded her, 'you wanted my help for another "nice girl" who had got herself arrested for murder. Don't tell me this young friend of yours—'

'Nothing of the sort. Told you she was a solicitor,' said Vera. She was a tall rather heavily built woman with thick dark hair now liberally sprinkled with grey, that in theory was confined in an old-fashioned bun at the back of her head but all too often escaped from the pins that should have confined it. 'Thing is she has a client who's in that unfortunate predicament.'

'And—?'

'Knows him personally. Says he's innocent,' said Vera cryptically.

Perhaps the oddest thing about this conversation was that Sir Nicholas had so far refrained from taking any part in it. 'On what grounds does she base that assumption?' Antony asked cautiously.

'Says he couldn't do a thing like that, not in his nature,' Vera told him.

That, as she might have guessed, provoked Maitland to protest. 'Vera, you can't . . . Uncle Nick, you're not going to let her get away with a statement like that?

Sir Nicholas had all this time been stretched out very much at his ease in his usual chair, but now he looked up and smiled at his nephew, who had risen in his agitation and was standing with his back to the empty grate. 'I must admit you have my sympathy, my dear boy,' he said, 'and I think Vera would agree that in her own days at the bar she would have found such a statement unconvincing. All the same—'

'Nicholas tells me your list could be arranged to give you a few days out of town,' said Vera, sticking grimly to her point.

'Oh well, if you're both going to gang up on me.' He ignored his uncle's look of pain at his choice of words. 'You know what I think about Chedcombe, nothing good ever came out of it . . . except you, Vera.' And indeed such changes as had occurred in the house in Kempenfeldt Square since her arrival had been only for the better.

'But look here,' – Maitland had by no means finished with his

8

argument – 'when was this chap arrested? You did say it was a man, didn't you?'

'A young man by the name of Oliver Linwood,' said Vera. 'Lisa tells me he was arrested at the end of last week.'

'Then the trial can't possibly come on until after the long vacation. So why—?'

'Preliminary consultation,' said Vera, sounding pleased with the phrase.

'And is there anything, anything at all, besides this feeling your friend has got, to make it worthwhile my going down at this stage? Even if I decide to accept the brief, which I take it is the idea behind all this.'

'Don't know enough about the circumstances,' Vera told him. 'Nice girl though,' she said again, 'shouldn't like to let her down.'

'Why me?' asked Maitland in an injured tone.

Sir Nicholas obviously felt it time to take a hand. 'Your known predilection for meddling—' he began.

'But there's nothing to go on, nothing to say that my meddling, as you call it, would do any good at all.'

'Antony.' Jenny's previous silence had been less of a surprise than Sir Nicholas's; she was always a better listener than a talker. She waited a moment until her husband turned and looked at her and she was sure she had his full attention. 'Suppose this young man *is* innocent?' she asked.

'Jenny love, there's no reason to think he is, except what this friend of Vera's says. And that's the oldest cliché in the world.'

'But suppose he is,' she insisted.

'Then I suppose—' he said reluctantly, but changed course in mid-sentence. 'This isn't a conspiracy to get me out of town?' he asked, looking from one to the other of his companions.

'Nothing of the sort. Lisa's heard me speak of you, and that's why she telephoned me about this,' said Vera.

'What's the girl's full name for heaven's sake?' It was capitulation, and he knew it as well as the rest of them, but he wasn't quite ready yet to give in gracefully.

'Lisa Traherne.'

'And you said she lived in—?'

'Madingley. Her husband's a farmer there. His name is Dominic.'

9

'And what does *he* think of this Linwood fellow?'

'I don't know. Why not ask him yourself?' she suggested with a kind of innocent cunning.

'Oh, very well, since you're all so set on it.' He smiled then and went back to his chair again and picked up his glass. 'But I still think you might have got a little more information for me, Vera.'

'Telephone call . . . expensive,' said Vera, bringing forcibly to Maitland's mind the days before she was married when such a thing had been a serious consideration for her. 'Don't know how Lisa and her husband are placed, or this client of hers.'

'No, I see.' He paused, thinking it out. 'I could get away on Thursday evening at a pinch,' he said, 'and be back here in time to tie things up before the vacation. Would that do?'

'Extremely well, I should think.' Having gained her point Vera seemed only too ready to change the subject. 'Are you and Jenny going to Yorkshire as usual?'

'We're creatures of habit,' said Antony lightly, and allowed the conversation to drift in another direction. But privately he was wondering why the information at Vera's disposal was so scant. If she was seriously concerned about Mrs Traherne's ability to pay a large phone bill, she could easily have called her back.

The same point had occurred to Jenny too, as became apparent when they were alone together later. It seemed to cause her a slight uneasiness, but perhaps that was only because he was going to be out of town for a few days. Sir Nicholas and Vera might have their reasons for feeling that Antony's occasional absence wasn't a bad thing, even though the whole of the Trinity term had passed quietly with none of the cases he had been involved in causing any difficulty with the police, and in theory Jenny would agree with them. But she'd miss him, he knew, as much as he would miss her. 'With any luck, love, I'll be back before the weekend,' he promised.

But he should have learned long before that predictions based mainly on optimism are seldom fulfilled.

Thursday, 17th July

I

It wasn't until lunch time the following Thursday that Maitland was able to question his uncle on the subject, about which he felt some quite natural curiosity. There was a table kept at their favourite restaurant, Astroff's, until one o'clock each day during term in case either of them wished to use it; it must be admitted that there were occasions when Antony, desiring privacy, made sure of Sir Nicholas's intentions before taking advantage of this, but that day he was anxious to talk to him and only too glad of the opportunity to do so alone.

Neither of them was in court that day, and Bill, the waiter who usually looked after them, didn't need telling what drinks they would find acceptable. But when these had been brought and their luncheon ordered, with a tacit understanding that it wouldn't appear immediately, Maitland wasted no time in broaching the subject that at the moment was foremost in his mind. 'This business of my going to Chedcombe, Uncle Nick, you can't tell me Vera doesn't know anything more than she told us about it.'

Uncharacteristically, Sir Nicholas made no direct reply. 'If I must tell you the truth my dear boy—' he began and broke off as though unsure as to how to finish the sentence.

'I should prefer it,' said Antony, allowing a certain dryness to be evident in his voice. A stranger observing them might have seen at that moment a certain elusive likeness between the two, though otherwise – except for their height – they were so very dissimilar in appearance.

Sir Nicholas was a man to whom the newspapers were fond of applying the description handsome, which had the worst effect on his temper, so that a conspiracy existed between Vera and Jenny

11

to remove any article which contained the offending word before he had a chance to see it. His hair was fair enough to make it impossible to tell whether it was yet going grey; he was much more heavily built than his nephew, though without any hint of stoutness; was very neat in his appearance where the younger man preferred to be casually dressed except when his profession demanded greater propriety; and generally spoke with an air of authority of which he was quite unconscious, though Antony might have been inclined to argue this last point, having heard his uncle dealing in the most dulcet manner with a nervous witness in court. Maitland, on the other hand, had dark hair that was generally inclined to be unruly except when it had been confined for some time under his wig in court, when it was some little time before it sprang up again into its usual disorder. He had a thin, intelligent face and a humorous look that would have told that same observant stranger a good deal about him – too much sense of humour for his own good certainly and, any of his friends would have added, too much sensitivity as well. An uncomfortable combination.

Sir Nicholas seemed to have made up his mind that his unfinished sentence didn't provide a sufficient answer to his nephew's query. 'If Jenny had known what this proposed client of yours was accused of she might not have been so willing to encourage you to go,' he said.

'Murder, I understood,' said Antony frowning. As an explanation it was rather less than adequate.

'Murder, yes. To be precise, of smothering a two-week-old baby.'

That brought Maitland up short. 'Yes, I see,' he said at last slowly. And then, 'In that case, why were you and Vera so anxious I should get involved, Uncle Nick? *Was* it just to get me out of London?'

'I have to agree that in the ordinary way that might have been an inducement,' said Sir Nicholas. He picked up his glass, sipped a little of the contents, and regarded his nephew rather seriously over the rim before putting it down again. 'You won't misunderstand me, Antony, neither of us wishes to dispense with your company—'

'You want to get me out of the way of this new Assistant

Commissioner at Scotland Yard,' said Maitland, interrupting without ceremony. 'It's no use, Uncle Nick, if he wants to make trouble he'll get his chance sooner or later.'

'Unfortunately,' said Sir Nicholas, diverted for the moment, 'that is only too true. If I could trust your discretion—'

'You ought to be able to by now. Or perhaps not,' he added, seeing his uncle's sceptical look. 'But isn't that really your only reason, because quite frankly I don't think it's good enough.'

'I think you should have seen for yourself, Antony, that Vera is seriously worried about this matter.'

'Yes, I gathered that, but—'

'She has a great affection for the young lady she spoke of, and also a good deal of trust in her judgement.'

'That also I had surmised.'

'I should have been astonished if you had not done so. The thing is, Antony,' he went on rather quickly as his nephew seemed about to interrupt, 'this Mrs Traherne made an appeal to Vera, and if she's right about the accused man they both certainly need the kind of help you can give them. The girl, Lisa, hasn't much experience of criminal matters.'

'It's odd,' said Maitland musingly. 'If the application had been made directly to me you would certainly have condemned me for entertaining it for a moment.' It was obvious that Sir Nicholas had some blistering comment ready for that, and he added in a hurry, 'Uncle Nick, you should have made your position quite clear to me.' He ventured to pause then and to his relief Sir Nicholas held his peace. 'You're as worried about Vera as I am about Jenny,' Antony added less forcefully. 'I mean, if I do decide to take the case, if these preliminary consultations Vera spoke of convince me it's necessary, the whole thing will inevitably be discussed at some time or another between the four of us.'

'We none of us want to hurt Jenny,' said his uncle. 'You know that, Antony, as well as I do. And I have to admit that this matter is very close to Vera's heart.' He stopped there and added with a smile, having apparently undergone one of those quick changes of mood that his nearest and dearest were so accustomed to, 'But before she had you . . . before she had Jenny to feel maternal about, I think this girl, Lisa . . . well, I think Vera had a very real affection for her.'

Antony would have liked to smile back, particularly in view of this rather less lucid than usual statement, but on the whole it might not have been altogether wise. He said instead, 'But suppose I find—'

'You know Vera. If it turns out that this friend of hers must face an unpleasant truth she'll accept it. But at least I think she'd like to be convinced of the necessity.'

'Yes, of course. I know that, Uncle Nick. But on the other hand, supposing this Lisa Traherne is right about her client. . . I'm sorry to keep harping on the subject, but in that case I can't refuse to discuss the matter with Jenny.'

'Of course not. If you accept the case I think we must leave that to Vera, my dear boy. The initial explanations at least.'

'We can both trust her,' said Antony, and this time he did permit himself a smile. 'Only you know how much losing the baby affected Jenny, Uncle Nick, and I always feel guilty about that because it happened because she was worried about me. And then to have the doctors tell her—'

'Don't underestimate Jenny either,' his uncle advised him. 'Anyone who's put up with you all these years must have considerably more strength of mind than you seem to be giving Jenny credit for.'

The conversation seemed in danger of getting out of hand again. 'Yes, there is that,' said Maitland rather vaguely. 'But I think you can understand, Uncle Nick, that on the whole I hope I find there's no case to investigate.'

'As you would say yourself, who lives may learn,' said Sir Nicholas, benevolent again. 'But don't try to persuade yourself, Antony . . . either way.'

'I hope I can promise you that. Anyway, now we've got that out of the way, what else does Vera know?'

'Only as much as Mrs Traherne told her on the telephone.'

'Why should this Oliver – whatever his name is – want to go about killing babies? Is he mad?'

'He may be for all I know, but as far as the prosecution's case goes the question doesn't arise. What do you know about Estates Tail?'

'Without looking at the details, not very much. Except that they were abolished by the Law of Property Act 1925, when they might be turned into Entailed Interests, and I think that at that time it was decided that personal property could be tied up as well as land. But whether new Entailed Interests can be created—'

'They can, but that's another point that's immaterial. Apparently the Linwoods are an old family, and the whole thing goes back a great number of years. Mrs Traherne will give you the details and the only point that need concern us at the moment is that theirs was a tail male. Oliver's cousin Walter inherited the estate – really these cases where all the protagonists have the same surname are quite impossible – but he died without issue at the beginning of last month. His wife, however, was pregnant.'

'I'm beginning to see.'

'So I should hope,' said Sir Nicholas austerely. Maitland forebore with difficulty from pointing out to him that if the case was not altogether to his liking he had no one to blame but himself. 'Being the only other male member of the family Oliver would have inherited if the child had turned out to be a girl. However, it was a boy called Mark, as I understand it after his grandfather, but he did not, as I told you, survive for very long.'

'Suffocated you say?'

'So I understand,' said Sir Nicholas again. 'Mrs Traherne will give you the details,' he added distastefully.

'But are they sure? A child that age . . . I always understood there were things called cot deaths, which are quite natural but not easily explained.'

'Well, it will be something for you to look into, but certainly the matter is being treated as one of murder. If, of course, you convince them otherwise . . . and it's no use asking me any more questions, Antony. I've told you all I know.'

'But is that the whole of the prosecution's case . . . motive?'

'I shouldn't suppose so for a moment, but as I've said twice you'll have to get the details from Mrs Traherne.' He turned his head and saw with satisfaction that Bill had intercepted his signal. 'Let us dismiss these unpleasant matters from our minds,' he suggested, 'and enjoy our meal. I understand from Vera that Jenny will be spending a good deal of time with us while you're gone, so you needn't be afraid she'll be lonely. What time does your train leave this evening for Chedcombe?'

II

Maitland dined on the train and wasn't expecting to be met. As he surrendered his ticket and left the platform at Chedcombe station he was wondering whether the Crown Court happened to be in session, and if it was, whether it was his duty to make his presence known to the President of the Bar Mess that evening. On the whole though he thought tomorrow would be soon enough, and a quiet drink in the lounge would be more to his taste, before he went up to his room and phoned Jenny to report his safe arrival. But the matter was decided for him by a young man who intercepted him as he started to cross the station yard. 'Mr Maitland?' he asked, and when Antony admitted the fact said merely, 'Dominic Traherne. My wife asked me to meet you.'

He was a dark young man, no more than two inches shorter than Maitland himself, slenderly built but with a sort of whipcord strength about him. 'That's very kind of you both,' Antony told him, 'but it's only a step to the George, and not dark yet.'

'Your luggage?'

'Just this one small case.' He was used to travelling light but felt no necessity to explain the reason, the old injury to his shoulder that made his right arm useless for such things as carrying heavy bags.

'And you know the place quite well, even though it's over three years since you were here,' said Dominic. 'And don't like it either, from what Miss Langhorne – I should say Lady Harding – tells us.' He smiled suddenly, disarmingly. 'The thing is,' he confided, 'Lisa asked me to find out if you'd mind talking to her this evening. She thought that however tired you were you'd say yes if she came herself, but you might not mind saying no to me.'

'I see.' He thought about it for a moment, but the sooner he reached a decision one way or another the better. 'Does that mean you want me to come out to Madingley with you?'

'We'd like that, of course, but it seems a bit thick at this time of the evening. As a matter of fact Lisa's waiting at the hotel, but she promised to keep out of sight unless you agreed to see her.'

16

'I'm looking forward to it,' said Maitland, not altogether accurately. 'I only got half a story from Vera . . . well, from my uncle actually. So I suppose it's high time I heard the rest of it.'

It took them only a few minutes to reach the George, a comfortable hostelry generally patronised by the gentlemen of the bar. Dominic slipped away to tell his wife that she had got her wish, leaving Maitland to sign the register. The manager, who remembered him from his previous visit, though fortunately he was a new man since the first disastrous occasion when Maitland had stayed there, came out to greet him, carefully concealing his curiosity as to what had brought him into the town a few days after the Crown Court sittings had moved on to Northdean. Maitland accepted his key, and left his case to be taken up to his room.

In the lounge he found Dominic and Lisa Traherne awaiting him. She'd made good use of her time by ensconcing herself in a corner where they were at a comfortable distance from their nearest neighbours. Chedcombe, being something of a show-place, had more than its share of visitors in the summer months, but fortunately only a few of them seemed to have chosen to stay in on that warm and pleasant evening.

Lisa looked younger than he had expected. If she had already been qualified and in practice before Vera married his uncle at the end of the Trinity term four years ago she must be twenty-seven or twenty-eight at least. But though she might look youthful there was plenty of character in her face, which was not exactly beautiful but very much more to his taste than mere prettiness would have been. She had very thick, soft, shiny hair, fair but by no means dazzlingly so, and looked just about as unlike a solicitor as anyone could.

Dominic got to his feet immediately. 'I'll leave you to it,' he said. 'You can find me in the bar when you're through. And you needn't be afraid of being neglected in here, I expect Henry saw you come in.'

'I expect so too.' But even as he spoke Antony had reached a decision. He was about to be regaled with Lisa's opinion of the accused man, and it would undoubtedly be useful to know what her husband thought of him too, and how much one of them had influenced the other in the matter of opinion. 'I wish you'd stay,' he said. 'As Linwood is a friend of both of you I'm sure you know as much about the case as Mrs Traherne does by now.'

'That's true, but I thought—'

'Forget it.' He divided a smile between the two of them. 'And here is Henry, as you predicted. He had a soft spot for Vera when she lived here and I think I still bask a little in her reflected glory.' He waited until they were alone again and then went on, 'I've an idea it may have been quite a blow to you when Vera left Chedcombe, Mrs Traherne, but I can't tell you what a difference she's made to our household. You may know that my wife and I have a flat at the top of my uncle's house in Kempenfeldt Square and Uncle Nick is one of those men who terrorise their equals but are as putty in the hands of the people supposed to be serving them. Vera somehow got on terms with his resident tyrants, and life has been very much simpler for all of us since then.'

Lisa, who had been eyeing him doubtfully, relaxed and smiled at him. 'I rather gather, Mr Maitland, that all this is a prelude to your wanting to find out something about Dominic and me.'

No use denying it. 'Am I so easily read?' Antony asked her in a rather teasing tone. 'You're quite right, of course, but how did you guess?'

'I think it stands to reason. You know nothing about Oliver, so for the moment you want to know how far you can accept our estimate of him. I warned Dominic that the one thing he mustn't say was that Oliver would never have done a thing like that, because I know you must have heard that a thousand times and disbelieved it nine hundred and ninety-nine of them. Only in this case – you'll see for yourself – it happens to be true.'

'Well, I shall have the opportunity of seeing for myself, shan't I?'

'Yes, I arranged for us to see him tomorrow morning if that's all right with you. Only . . . oh, you'll want to make up your own mind, I know that. But I'd be willing to bet he's not like anyone else you've ever met.'

'You're beginning to intrigue me,' said Antony lightly. 'But you were going – remember? – as you so rightly guessed I wanted, to tell me something about yourselves.'

'To begin with I think it would be awfully nice if you dropped the Mr and Mrs Traherne. It's such a mouthful, and Lisa and

Dominic will do quite well if you don't mind being on first name terms with us. It doesn't commit you to anything,' she added hurriedly.

'Thank you.' He was glad to know that Vera had made that much at least clear to her, that his coming to Chedcombe didn't necessarily guarantee his acceptance of the brief. 'I know, of course, that you're a solicitor, and may become my instructing solicitor if we both decide to go ahead with that, but what about your husband?'

'I'm a farmer,' said Dominic promptly. 'You mentioned Madingley, so obviously you know that's where we live. I have four hundred acres, not my own land, I'm a tenant of the Linwoods.'

'Oliver Linwood's tenant?'

'Yes, now I suppose I am, but everything's happened so quickly I haven't really had time to take it in. It certainly doesn't prejudice my opinion of Oliver, whom I've known all my life.'

'And how long have you known him, Lisa?'

'Since Dominic and I were married, which oddly enough was almost exactly the same time as Vera's wedding. In fact she hardly knows Dominic, except that I introduced them when we were first engaged.'

'Four years then?'

'Almost exactly. I've lived all my life in Chedcombe, my father's a solicitor here and I'm his partner. We changed the firm's name when I married, because he thought Williams & Traherne sounded better than Williams & Williams.'

'He must, if you'll pardon me for saying so, have considerably more experience than you have. Why didn't he take on Oliver Linwood's defence?'

Lisa glanced at her husband and then back at Maitland again. 'Because he doesn't believe him,' she said. 'He'll advise me, of course, but I felt, and Dominic agrees with me, that believing in the person you're defending is more than half the battle. That's why I was anxious that Vera would be able to persuade you—?'

'Because I have a reputation for being credulous?'

'Now you're laughing at me,' she said without resentment. 'Because I thought you'd listen at least, and I was very sure how you'd make up your mind.'

19

'Very well then, I'm listening.'

She hesitated for a moment. 'I'd better tell you a little bit about Oliver first,' she said. 'Dominic's known him all his life, as he said, in fact they're practically the same age. I only met him after I went to live in Madingley after we were married. Country life was rather strange to me at first, though I've come to like it very much, and we fell into the habit of going down to the pub most evenings after dinner. The Saracen's Head that is, though I've never been able to find anyone who could tell us how it got that name. It seems very unlikely . . . but that's beside the point. I think it was Dominic's idea of keeping me from becoming bored' – the glance she gave her husband was full of affection and Antony found himself warming towards her, and for the first time hoping, though still not very wholeheartedly, that she wasn't going to be disillusioned – 'and as a matter of fact there's generally some amusing talk going on. If Oliver happens to be there we generally sit with him, and there's an older man, the editor of the Chedcombe Herald to be exact, who's there most evenings. He's a widower, and I expect he's lonely. We just have a natter, and then go home. I didn't tell you we live in the cottage that Dominic's father left him in the village. He prefers that to the farmhouse that goes with the land he rents, so that's been divided into two . . . I suppose you could call them tied cottages.'

'So you feel you know Oliver Linwood pretty well?'

'Yes I do, and he's the last person in the world . . . but that's something you'll have to decide for yourself. I suppose actually we ought to tell you something about the Linwood family, as the Estates Tail seem to be germane to the issue.'

'I suppose you should.'

'Well, Dominic can do that better than I can.'

'So long as you chip in with the legal bits,' said Dominic obligingly. 'The family tree, so far as it concerns us, isn't really very complicated. How far do you want me to go back?'

'1925 seems to be as good a date as any.' Lisa nodded approvingly, rather as though, Antony thought with amusement, she'd been afraid he hadn't done his homework on the subject.

'That would be – let's see – Oliver's grandfather, for whom he was named. I don't mean he was the only member of the family living at that time, but he had inherited the estate, I don't know exactly when. But why 1925?'

'I take it,' said Maitland, looking at Lisa for confirmation, 'that the estate was already entailed and that he converted it in that year.'

'Yes, of course, and a very silly business it is to my mind,' said Lisa, suddenly looking rather pugnacious. 'Not only did he continue it in the male line, but he added his personal property to the new entailed interest.'

'But it didn't matter as it happened,' said Dominic placatingly. 'He only had sons, and they only had sons, so there was no question of defrauding the female line.'

'It wouldn't have been fraud,' said Lisa, who obviously liked to get these things straight, 'just very unfair. And it was unfair anyway because it meant that the eldest son got everything.'

'When did grandfather die?'

'That was before my time,' said Dominic, 'but I remember my father saying that Mark Linwood, that was the eldest son, had inherited when he was only twenty-five.'

'I've researched the dates,' said Lisa, 'because I knew Oliver wouldn't have the faintest idea except where it concerned him directly.' She seemed to have forgotten that her husband was supposed to be the expert on the Linwood family. 'Oliver had two sons, Mark who was born in 1910—'

'Which seems to make grandfather's death 1935,' said Maitland, who had fished a rather tattered envelope from his pocket and was beginning to scrawl a few notes on it.

'I suppose so, if it's important. The younger son was called Andrew and was born in 1913. He was at university when his father died and I suppose, though I don't know this for a fact, that Mark paid for him to continue his education. Anyway he became a doctor and practised in the village here.'

'If it's of any interest he brought me into the world,' said Dominic. 'I don't remember him though, he died in 1948. Too early to have accumulated much in the way of capital. His wife Millicent, and Oliver who was two years old at the time, moved into a small house, and managed somehow though I think they were always fairly hard up.'

'Is Mrs Andrew Linwood still alive?'

'No, she died in 1968.'

'Did Oliver ever tell you anything about his financial arrangements after that, Dominic?'

'He asked my advice when he sold the house and went to live in that practically derelict cottage in Church Row. Since then he's been existing somehow, on very little money.'

'Perhaps he had an allowance from his cousin Walter.'

'I'm pretty sure he wouldn't have accepted help from him.'

'Walter, I take it, was from the senior side of the family?'

'Yes he was Mark's son, I've known him all my life too, as a matter of fact he was born exactly two months before Oliver was.' Dominic had taken over the narrative again. 'Mark Linwood and his wife Maude were killed together in an air crash in 1967. I remember that date very clearly, because it was naturally something of a sensation here.'

'Did Walter have any profession?'

'No, it was always understood that he'd learn the details of running the estate and take over from his father in due course. Only he died a little over a month ago, and that's what has caused all the trouble.'

'What was wrong?' Maitland was studying his notes, which even to him were not very legible. 'He can't have been more than about twenty-nine.'

'Apparently he'd had a heart defect from a child. You'd have to ask the doctor for details, but it was generally understood in the village that he died of a heart attack.'

'It isn't important anyway,' said Lisa a little impatiently. 'Sandra, his wife, was pregnant, and his son was born post-humously on the twenty-fifth of June.'

'It was rather like a lottery really,' said Dominic. 'I mean, if it had been a daughter Oliver would have scooped the pool.'

'Yes, I understand that.' Antony smiled at him. 'Well the financial motive is clear enough, but—'

'Don't you see?' Lisa interrupted him. 'I don't think Oliver would be capable of killing a fly, let alone a baby, under any circumstances. But financial considerations would be the last thing that would ever induce him to do so.'

'From what you tell me he was living in rather reduced circumstances. What is his occupation?'

'He doesn't have one, that's one of the things the police think terribly suspicious. When there's a concert in Chedcombe, or the local choral society are doing *Messiah* or anything like that, he attends for the local paper and writes a review, but you can imagine how much that brings in and anyway I think he only does it to get a free ticket because he's mad about music. I told you he isn't like anybody else. Some people say he's lazy, because nobody denies his intelligence, but really it's just that he doesn't care about material things at all. He lives the way he likes, and he doesn't want anything different.'

'Yes, I can quite see that the police, and perhaps any jury we come up against eventually, would find that hard to understand,' said Maitland thoughtfully. 'All the same I suppose there's more to the case against your friend than merely motive.'

'Oh yes, he was there, at Linwood House I mean. I'd better put it in order for you,' said Lisa. 'Walter died on the ninth of June and the baby – Sandra decided to call him after his grandfather – came on June twenty-fifth. She had rather a long labour, and the doctor said she shouldn't be moved, so the birth took place at home. Anyway there was a nurse in attendance, and she stayed on to look after things. The eighth of July was a beautiful day, and the nurse put him out in his pram to take the air. That was at about two o'clock, and at two-thirty she went into the house to help Sandra dress. She was still spending the mornings in bed because the doctor said she needed all the rest she could get after the bad time she'd had. It was three-fifteen when the nurse came out again, and the first thing she did, of course, was look at the baby, and he was dead.'

'Asphyxia, I understand, is rather difficult to detect, and particularly in a child of that age.'

'Yes, the pathologist's report is full of long words and I expect you'll want to see it yourself, but there wasn't really much room for mistake. Little Mark was still lying on his back, but the pillow had been pulled from under his head and placed over his face. There was absolutely no way he could have got into that position himself.'

'No, I see. You said Oliver Linwood was there?'

'Yes, he had a snack at the Saracen's Head that lunch time, which is another reason the police suspected Oliver because that was an expense he didn't usually incur, though he quite often had

23

his evening meal with Ruth and Tom Jenkins who own the pub. I think – though I'm not actually certain – that they gave him a special price, eating with the family. Afterwards he decided to walk up to the house to see how Sandra was doing, and he rang the front door bell just before three o'clock.'

'That raises a few questions. First, where was the pram?'

'On the terrace to the right of the front door. He could easily have walked over and looked at the baby, but he says he didn't. Just went straight up the drive to the house.'

'Then, what time does the Saracen's Head close?'

'Two o'clock. You're going to ask me how long the walk would have taken him, certainly not more than half an hour. He says he didn't go home, only he didn't think Sandra would be ready to receive visitors much before three – which was true enough – so he dawdled on the way. I know it doesn't sound good,' Lisa added rather defensively.

Antony ignored the opportunity for comment. 'Did he see anybody as he went?' he asked.

'Nobody after he had left the main street in the village, and asking around I haven't been able to find anyone who saw him either.'

'Let's get back to the doorstep of Linwood House then. He rang the bell, and was admitted I suppose.'

'Yes, after no more time than it took Hilda – that's the housemaid – to get from the kitchen quarters.'

'I didn't know anybody had a housemaid now.'

'This is an old-fashioned village, Mr Maitland. Hilda's mother and grandfather were both in service at Linwood House in different capacities. Perhaps the connection even goes back before that, I don't know. Anyway these things seem almost to go by heredity here.'

'I see. So Hilda let Mr Linwood in. I shall have to call him Oliver, it's too confusing otherwise.'

'Yes, of course. She took him into the drawing-room, and Sandra joined him a moment later.'

'Where was the nurse at that time? What's her name anyway?'

'Dora Tompkins. She says she was in Sandra's room clearing up, which wasn't strictly her job but I think she's a woman with a sense of order, and Sandra is used to being looked after and never thought anything of asking her to undertake jobs like that.'

'I was wondering, you see, from which windows of the house the pram could be seen.'

'Not from upstairs certainly, and not from the drawing-room either unless someone had craned out of the window and looked along the front of the house. Miss Tompkins placed it in a sheltered corner, Sandra's inclined to blame her but it was her fault really for wanting so much attention, and nobody could possibly have thought any harm could come to the baby there.'

'All the same, on such a hot day the drawing-room window would certainly be open. Oliver must have been there from three o'clock, wouldn't he have heard footsteps if anyone had walked along the terrace?'

'I asked him that. He says he didn't, but he's awfully vague about things and I can quite imagine if he was lost in some train of thought he wouldn't have noticed if a herd of elephants went by. Anyway he was only alone for a few minutes, then Sandra joined him and I suppose they were talking. They might not have noticed either.'

'Yes, I see that. All the same, if Oliver's telling the truth the period between two-thirty and three o'clock seems to be the most likely time. What is it like just outside Linwood House?'

'The grounds have always been kept in perfect order, but nobody's done anything to alter their layout for hundreds of years I should say. You know there was always a shrubbery where the ladies of the house took their exercise in the bad weather. That's still there, not more than ten or twelve yards I should say from where the pram was left.'

'Come now, that's encouraging,' Antony told her. 'It couldn't have taken more than a moment or two to kill the poor child. Someone could have nipped in and out of the bushes without too much difficulty . . . unless there were any gardeners about?'

'There's an old man and his grandson, but they were both working at the other side of the grounds behind the house.'

'That's a pity. Mrs Traherne – I'm sorry, Lisa – who else besides your friend could possibly have had a motive?'

'For killing Mark Linwood, nobody.'

If Maitland had seemed vague at first there was no question that he was alert now. Dominic, watching from the sidelines and a countryman at heart, had an incongruous vision of a hound catching the first whiff of the scent of his quarry. 'That's rather an odd way of putting it,' Antony said. 'Could you explain it to me?'

'Yes, of course. There have been two cases in Chedcombe of infants being kidnapped, and then found dead. Smothered.'

'How long ago?'

'On the twentieth and the twenty-third of June.'

'Do you mean to say the police made no connection?'

'They think they know who did it, a girl called Henrietta Vaughan.'

'Even so—'

'She's what's called nowadays an unmarried mother, and her baby, a boy, was born dead on the thirteenth of June. She was released from the hospital a few days later, nothing physically wrong with her, but the police have since decided that the experience deranged her altogether. She lived in Chedcombe, those two cases were in Chedcombe, and they just don't think there's any connection with what happened to the baby at Madingley, particularly as such a good motive – to their mind – exists. In fact, I rather think they believe those two first cases gave Oliver the idea.'

'All the same . . . have you seen the girl, have you seen the parents of the two other dead babies?'

'I thought that would be something you'd like to do yourself, supposing you decide to take the case.'

Maitland grinned at that. 'Like is hardly the word,' he said, 'though I admit in that event I should certainly need to see them. However, that will wait. I must talk to your client first, you did say tomorrow morning, didn't you?'

'Yes, I did. I'll pick you up here at ten o'clock if that will suit you.' She stood up and added with the air of one deliberately anticipating the worst, 'That will give you plenty of time to have lunch with us and catch the afternoon train back to London if that's what you decide to do.' She paused, and glanced at Dominic as though there might be some strength to be derived merely by looking at him, and then went on. 'I know it must seem an awfully strange story to you, Mr Maitland, but I think perhaps when you've seen Oliver for yourself you may agree with us.'

26

'Perhaps I shall.' Antony was on his feet too but he had a suggestion to make. 'Why don't you sit down, both of you, and have another drink. Even if one of you – Dominic I suppose? – has to drive back to Madingley I don't think that will put you in a state of intoxication. And we should at least get to know one another a little better.'

III

It was nearly eleven o'clock when he got up to his room and put through his call to Jenny. She answered promptly, and told him she had not been upstairs for long, after dining with Sir Nicholas and Vera. 'What about your case, Antony? Will you be home for the weekend?'

'I can't possibly tell you yet, love. I'm torn two ways as it is. They're a nice couple, this friend of Vera's who wants my help and her husband. It's a queer thing, I keep thinking I've met her before, but I'm quite sure I've never set eyes on her any of the times I've been in Chedcombe.'

'One of those tribal likenesses I suppose,' said Jenny. 'Antony—'

'Yes, love?'

'Vera told me what it's all about.'

'I see.' For the moment he couldn't think of any other comment, even though that seemed inadequate.

'She seems to have a great deal of confidence in Lisa's judgement,' said Jenny. 'And you know, Antony' – the unspoken memory of her own experience remained unspoken between them, but perhaps after so many years there was no need for words – 'if she's right, I don't think you should hesitate. You should do what you can to help.'

They talked for nearly a quarter of an hour after that but the matter wasn't mentioned again. All the same, by the time he replaced the receiver Antony was feeling strangely comforted, even with the realisation that he would be visiting his prospective client in prison the following day.

Friday, 18th July

I

Chedcombe is a town that prides itself on its atmosphere. The market square, of which the George Hotel can quite fairly be regarded as an ornament, is still cobbled, and though the weekly market has now been banished to a more convenient spot it must look very much as it has done for the past several hundred years. It was Antony's considered opinion that there were probably more antique shops in the town than anywhere else of comparable size in Britain. The stream which meandered through the square was infrequently bridged and must cause considerable inconvenience to shoppers, but nobody had ever been known to voice a complaint. The visitors thought it quaint, and the townspeople – even those who gained no financial benefit from the influx of tourists – had long since become reconciled to it.

In such a place it was not to be expected that a modern prison would be countenanced, and the building stood well outside the town. Lisa picked him up on exactly the stroke of ten and Maitland would have been glad enough to make the journey in silence. Of all the aspects of his profession this was the one that displeased him most, and he was endeavouring to banish the thought of the interview to come from his mind by thinking of the first time he had made this journey and how different the countryside looked now in high summer from on that day eleven years before when he had made it in mid-winter. The consequences of that first journey had been unexpected to say the least and, along with the attitude of the townspeople towards the girl who had become his client, had given him an extreme distaste for Chedcombe and all its works. But he didn't know Lisa well enough yet to make the trip in silence and presently roused himself to say, 'I've been out here before, as Vera probably told you, but I don't know the names of any of the villages we're passing. Is Madingley in this direction?'

'No, you take South Street out of the square, and then it's down a turning off the Northdean Road. Quite a pretty place. People always say it must be lovely in summer, and of course it is, but I've come to love it just as much at any time of the year. If you do stay over the weekend you must come and see us. In any case,' she added in rather a doubtful tone, 'I expect you'd want to see the scene of the crime.'

Antony turned his head and smiled at her, though he doubted if she saw it as she was very properly concentrating on the winding road they were driving along. 'I can't say that last is much of an inducement,' he said, 'though it may of course be necessary. I'd be very happy to visit you and Dominic in any case.'

'I'm glad you're with me anyway this morning,' she confided. 'I haven't seen Oliver since the Magistrates' Court hearing, and seeing someone you know so well in prison is . . . well, shall we say embarrassing at the very least.'

'I can quite see it must be,' said Maitland, who had his own reasons for disliking their errand but no desire at all to speak of them. 'And embarrassing for Linwood too, I suppose.'

He was still looking at her, and this time she smiled though she still didn't take her eyes from the road. 'I very much doubt it,' she said. 'Oliver . . . I told you he isn't like anybody else. I shouldn't think he'll display any of what people might call the proper emotions at the predicament he finds himself in.'

'I don't know about you,' said Maitland, 'but on the whole I find that encouraging.' But he was glad she didn't challenge him as to what he meant by that.

They talked of other things then and presently reached the prison. If Lisa had been dreading this moment there was no sign of it. She explained their errand composedly enough and presently they found themselves in the interview room allotted to them, which he could have sworn was the same one that he had seen on the previous occasions he had visited this rather dreary place, a smallish room with a shiny wood table faintly overlaid by dust, and several hard chairs. But all such places have a certain similarity and he strolled to the window to verify the impression, looking out through the bars to where the land fell away steeply towards the river.

There were willows there in full leaf, and the meadows were lush, not flooded as the first time he had seen them. A freak of memory brought to his mind the words that had occurred to him then . . . one saw the mud, the other the stars . . . but even the stars couldn't be very consoling when the door was locked by someone other than yourself. A pleasant place to rot in, he thought bitterly, and for a moment he was horrified by the impression that he might have spoken the words aloud. But when he turned Lisa was already sitting at the table, as composed as she had been before. She had laid out a foolscap pad in front of her together with a ballpoint pen. 'Shall I make notes, or would you rather?' she asked.

'I expect I have an old envelope somewhere, if anything arises on which I think my memory may need jogging,' he assured her. 'For the rest, I shall be relying on you.' And perhaps because he realised the bare room and the prison precincts had aroused in him an unwelcome feeling of sympathy he added rather roughly, 'If it comes to that.'

To his surprise she flushed at his words but her eyes were still steady. 'I haven't forgotten we're on probation,' she assured him.

'I didn't exactly—'

'You didn't mean to be unkind, but it's true all the same, isn't it? Don't worry, Mr Maitland,' (he recognised as she spoke that it was ridiculous that she should be reassuring him) 'you don't know Oliver and I can't expect you to make up your mind on my opinion and Dominic's.'

'I'm sorry—' Maitland started; but he wasn't quite sure how the sentence would have ended, and perhaps it was just as well that the door opened at that moment and Oliver Linwood came in.

For once in his life, perhaps because what Lisa and Dominic had told him had aroused his curiosity, Maitland was conscious only of the man who had entered, not of the closing of the door behind him or the presence of the warder in the corridor outside. Linwood's eyes were perhaps two inches below his own, which meant he must be almost exactly Dominic's height, but the prisoner looked taller because of his extreme thinness; not an unhealthy slenderness, but not muscular either. His hair was straight and mouse-coloured, rather longer than suited Maitland's taste, though he realised immediately that this might be of deliberate purpose or simply because getting a haircut was something too unimportant to remember. The fact that it was also very clean and well brushed didn't fit exactly with the rest of his appearance. His suit was old and had obviously never been well-fitting; his collar also clean but a little frayed around the neckline; his scuffed shoes suede with nothing at all to recommend them except that they were probably very comfortable by now. As for his face, it was thin like the rest of him, and it was only when Antony tried to describe him later that he realised he had no really outstanding features at all, not a man you would give a second glance to. On appearance alone, a very ordinary sort of chap.

Lisa scrambled to her feet. 'Oliver dear,' she said, 'this is Mr Maitland, the counsel I hope is going to represent you.'

Linwood turned his attention to Antony and smiled at him. The smile lent more character to his face. It was pleasant enough but had a hint of the sardonic about it. 'I'm pleased to meet you, of course,' he said, 'because we've all heard all about you in this part of the world, and I suppose I'm as curious as the next man. What exactly does Lisa mean, though, that she hopes you're going to represent me? I thought that was your job.'

'If I accept the brief,' said Antony, and stopped there because he had a strong feeling that the other man didn't need any further explanation.

'Lisa has told you no doubt that I wouldn't hurt a fly, which is one of her favourite expressions, but you're not so sure,' said Oliver. 'Sit down,' he added, turning to her, 'there's a good girl. If we're going to talk we may as well make ourselves comfortable.' He seemed to have no awareness at all of the incongruity of this remark as applied to the rather penitential chairs provided in the room.

Lisa seated herself and Linwood followed her example. Antony came across to the chair he would normally have taken, and stood behind it resting his hands lightly on the back. He didn't sense in this man the need for reassurance which was usually evident on such occasions. Linwood was obviously quite in control of the

31

situation, and if he was any judge would need very little encouragement to talk. 'Mrs Traherne has been good enough to outline to me the case against you,' Antony said. 'I gather you wish to plead Not Guilty—'

'I certainly do!'

'—but I'm sure she's also explained to you that a simple denial wouldn't have much chance of being believed in court. She would like some further investigation of the matter, and unless I'm willing to undertake this I doubt if she'd want to brief me at all. So you see I'm on probation as much as you are.'

Linwood considered this for a moment. 'It's all nonsense, you know,' he said at last. 'I had the opportunity if I'd wanted to take it, but what they're really resting their case on is motive, and that doesn't make sense.'

'You'll have to explain that to me, I'm afraid.'

Linwood spread his hands. 'I don't want the money,' he said simply. 'What should I do with it?'

'I can think of a number of things,' said Maitland rather dryly.

'Now you're making the mistake of going by appearances,' Oliver told him. 'You think I need a new suit, but this one is good for quite a few years yet and I do have one to change into when it goes to the cleaners. As for the rest . . . you know me Lisa, have I ever seemed to you to be hankering after the fleshpots?'

'No,' she admitted. 'But it isn't what I think that matters, it's what the jury will believe. And when they know how you live—'

'You leave my way of life out of it,' said Oliver amiably. 'I have enough for my simple needs and I like the way I live. What would I do with a fortune? Wear myself into a decline in case I lost it on the stock exchange. That isn't my idea of fun at all.'

'It isn't only the money,' Maitland reminded him. 'There's the estate as well.'

Oliver regarded him for a long moment. When he spoke it was difficult to believe that his sorrowful air was assumed. 'Don't you understand? That just makes things a thousand times worse. There's rather a lot of actual cash as a matter of fact, but I suppose it would be possible in theory to put it in the bank and forget about it. But what would I be doing managing an estate the size of Walter's?'

'A lot of people employ an agent to do the work for them. I

suppose if you're not interested in the financial aspect his salary wouldn't worry you.'

Linwood's manner was now definitely reproachful. 'I don't annoy easily,' he said, 'though I think you're deliberately trying to stir me up. But where does that get them? The people who employ agents, I mean. The wretched man would forever be wanting consultations. I should have to fly the country and I don't want to do that. I like living in England, and particularly I like living in Madingley.'

'I see.'

'The way you say that means you don't at all. All the same, it's true. What do you think I was doing at Linwood House that day?'

'Suppose you tell me.'

'I wanted to reassure Sandra that I was terribly glad young Mark hadn't turned out to be a girl. I'd have looked after them both in any case, and she could have stayed in the house, but of course that didn't arise, I just wanted to make sure she knew I wasn't harbouring any ill feelings.'

'And what had Mrs Linwood to say to that?'

'I never got the chance to tell her. We started out with a certain amount of chit-chat, and before I could get down to the subject there was that Tompkins woman shrieking her head off that she'd found the baby dead. And after that all hell broke loose, as you can imagine.'

'Yes . . . I see,' said Maitland again slowly. 'Tell me exactly your actions on that occasion. You left the Saracen's Head at closing time, I suppose.'

'Yes, two o'clock. And as Lisa's been on at me about how long it took me to walk up to Linwood House I suppose it's important. It was a nice day, and I walked about a bit before I got up my nerve. Sandra isn't my favourite person as a matter of fact.'

'And did you see anybody during these wanderings of yours?'

'Not after I left the village. When I walked up the drive I saw the pram, of course, but I'm not sentimental about babies and I can't say I was tempted to go over and look at my new cousin. And I didn't see any suspicious characters sneaking away into the shrubbery. I didn't notice the time then, I don't wear a watch. Time is just another interference with one's liberty, but as far as we could work it out later I rang the bell just before three o'clock.'

'We? Do you mean yourself and Mrs Walter Linwood?'

'Sandra? Oh, no. That was hardly the time to be asking her questions like that. I meant the local bobby, I told him exactly where I'd walked and we timed it out as well as we could. That's what we came up with.'

'That reminds me.' Maitland glanced at Lisa Traherne. 'Who is the investigating officer?'

'Detective Chief Inspector Camden.'

'That's a pity. I know the chap, that's all,' Antony added quickly seeing her anxious look. 'I don't think, to borrow Mr Linwood's phrase, that I'm his favourite person either.'

'Does that mean you'd rather not become involved?' Lisa was nothing if not blunt.

'Not really. I'd faced that possibility before I ever got on the train to come down here. And as Mr Linwood is already under arrest the police attitude will hardly make any difference to us. In fact it may even be a help if I can make him show his antagonism in court.'

'That means—?'

'Nothing at all just yet. Let's just go on with this question and answer business and see where it gets us. Mr Linwood may get tired of it before I do.'

'All right.' Lisa was obviously unwilling to give up the hope he had raised. 'What are you wanting him to tell you next?'

'We were talking about his visit to Linwood House the day the child was killed.'

'Nurse Tompkins came in and had hysterics,' said Oliver, taking up his narrative readily enough. 'As soon as I could get some sense out of her I went into what had been Walter's study to phone the police and they took over from there.'

'What about Sandra? I really can't distinguish all you Linwoods from one another unless I get into Christian names,' he added apologetically.

'Sandra rushed out onto the terrace and picked young Mark up and brought him inside. When I went back to the drawing-room he was lying on the sofa, and Tompkins seemed to have recovered a bit. She was gulping, and there was a red mark on her face, so I daresay Sandra had slapped her. Anyway both she and Sandra had a go at reviving the baby but it was no use.'

'If the body had been moved—?'

'Tompkins swore she hadn't touched him, but she agreed with Sandra that he was lying on his back in the pram with the pillow pulled from under his head and pressed over his face. Poor little devil,' he added feelingly.

'This was on July the eighth I believe?'

'Yes. They let me go home after a while, but I was arrested that same evening.'

'You had, however, had time to talk to the local constable in the meantime?'

'Yes, I told you that. He's a good chap and I think his idea was to warn me what was in the wind.'

'How do you mean?'

'Well as soon as she saw Camden alone Sandra had quite a story to tell him, I gathered, about me and my way of life. Biggins knows me—'

'Biggins being the local man?'

'Yes, that's right. So when he told me things might go as far as my arrest we talked about how long it had taken me to get to the house and it's light so late at this time of year we were able to go over the ground. It was after that that Camden and his minions took me in charge, but as I've learned a thing or two from Lisa, as I suspect you've gathered, I insisted on talking to her first. She told me not to say anything at all.'

'They'd already arrested him,' said Lisa. 'It wasn't a matter of answering questions and perhaps preventing that from happening.'

'I understand exactly. Camden was always impulsive, but I have to admit on the face of it he had reason on his side.'

Lisa gave him rather a sharp look, as though to say, are you changing your mind again? Maitland, interpreting the glance correctly, thought how much simpler it was to work with his old friend Geoffrey Horton, who would never have misinterpreted the sudden sharpness of his tone. 'Let's leave the facts for the moment then,' he suggested. 'Tell me something about yourself, Mr Linwood.'

'I can almost hear Counsel for the Prosecution asking me, what is your occupation?' said Oliver ruefully. 'If I describe myself as a gentleman of leisure do you think that would satisfy him?'

'Frankly, I doubt it. However I'd rather go back a little further than that. Your grandfather was your namesake, Oliver Linwood, and your father was his younger son?'

'Yes, that's right. Grandfather died in 1935, and my Uncle Mark took over the running of the estate.'

'I've been wondering about that. Do you understand about Estates Tail?'

Oliver grimaced. 'Lisa has explained it all to me at length,' he said. 'It seems, if I may say so, one of the things that might prompt a man to say the law's a hass.'

'They were abolished by the Law of Property Act in 1925,' said Maitland, 'at which time they might be made into entailed interests if the holder of the estate so wished.'

'I don't see the slightest difference between them if you must know,' said Oliver rather impatiently.

'There was one slight difference, that personal as well as real property might be added,' Maitland explained. 'In a way I'm inclined to agree with you about the undesirability of the whole arrangement, but that isn't the point at the moment. Two things are puzzling me. One is why your grandfather converted the entail, and the other is why he joined his personal property to the actual estate. He had two sons, and I gather your father was left completely dependent on his brother.'

'Yes, and to tell you the truth I wonder about that sometimes myself,' said Oliver. 'But it was all a long time ago, and I don't see how we can ever know for sure now.'

'Give me your best guess then. Have a stab at it,' he encouraged when Linwood hesitated.

'All right. I think it was because my Uncle Mark was very like Grandfather, and perhaps his favourite. I never knew the old man of course, but everything I've heard of him makes me think he was cut out by nature for running a large estate, and if that's so Uncle Mark obviously took after him. Whereas my father probably seemed to both of them a little unworldly. He wasn't really, though Mother always told me he was completely devoted to his profession. But it wasn't his fault he died so early, and if he hadn't he'd have provided for her perfectly well.'

'And for you too, I suppose.'

36

'Oh yes, that goes without saying, but you must have realised by now that wouldn't have mattered much to me. Only my Mother . . . she only died seven years ago, you know, and it was very hard on her.'

At this point Maitland pulled out the chair and sat down, and took the tattered envelope on which he had made yesterday's notes from his pocket. 'Your father's name was Andrew and he was a doctor,' he said, deciphering slowly his own scrawl. 'He was born in 1913 and died in 1948, which must have made him thirty-five at the time. What was the cause of his early death?'

'This is all hearsay evidence you know, I was only two at the time. But it seems to have been the same congenital weak heart that caught up with my cousin Walter six weeks or so ago.'

'And after your father's death . . . I'm afraid if I'm to help you I'll have to know all about your financial position,' he said in answer to Linwood's rather blank look.

'I wish I could make you understand that I'm not interested in money,' Oliver complained.

'You're going to have to persuade the jury so you might as well try out your story on me.'

'You don't look to me like a particularly mercenary man.'

'I don't think I am . . . particularly. All the same, if someone offered me a million pounds I can think of things I'd do with it,' Antony told him. 'And as I think that applies to most people—'

'Not to me. To me it seems a completely unnatural outlook,' Linwood protested. 'However if you think it will help for me to go into all the sordid details—'

'Take my word for it, it may not help but it's completely necessary.'

'From what Mother told me when my father died he had no more than about a couple of thousand pounds in the bank. The house we lived in was rented from the widow of the doctor who previously practised in Madingley. He'd been dead for several years, so it wasn't a case of taking over his list of patients, most of them had started to go elsewhere. But my father seems to have been popular in the village and that soon remedied itself. You never knew my Uncle Mark of course, Lisa. I wouldn't call him a sentimental man, and I don't think he cared a fig for my father, but he did care for the family name. So he bought a small house in the village for my mother and I wouldn't mind betting he hoped she'd marry again and thus be taken off his hands. He didn't let her starve, but there wasn't much to spare, I can tell you. Mother wasn't a stupid woman, you know, she'd have been quite capable of taking a job if I hadn't needed looking after, but she told me once that Uncle Mark made it a condition that she should do no work of any kind that would have been demeaning for a Linwood. As long as she didn't he'd look after us within reason and see to my education. He'd even have sent me to university, but I rather jibbed at that. It seemed such a waste of time.'

Maitland consulted his notes again. 'I see here that your uncle died in an air crash in 1967,' he said.

'Yes, he and my aunt Maude.'

'And after that?'

'My cousin Walter, who is just two months older than I am though he behaves sometimes as if he were nearer fifty, went on as before. But it was only for a year or just over, because Mother died in 1968. I couldn't see myself taking an allowance from Walter, we never got on, and things were worse than ever after he got married. So I asked Dominic's advice . . . this was long before you knew him, Lisa, but he was a sensible chap even then. He organised the sale of the house for me, which fetched far more than I expected, and invested the proceeds. I just retained enough to buy the cottage, which cost about tuppence ha'penny—'

'And which you have done nothing to improve,' Lisa put in rather tartly.

'Well . . . no. But even I can see that a roof over your head is important. Anyway, thanks to Dominic's level-headedness I have a minuscule income, and I do some music reviews for the local rag which gets me into the concerts free, and Martin will always take an article from me on country life if I'm particularly hard up, so I get by very well.'

'You didn't like your cousin Walter?'

'He disapproved of me,' said Oliver simply. Maitland made no immediate attempt to speak so when the silence had lengthened a little he asked, 'Well, what's the verdict?'

'If we went into court tomorrow I'm afraid I know what the

jury would say.'

'Yes, that isn't what I meant.'

'I know.' It wasn't the moment of decision because he had already made up his mind, but it was the moment when he must commit himself and he didn't relish it at all. 'Mrs Traherne is quite right,' he said, 'the matter must be looked into.'

'By you?' asked Lisa quickly.

'Who else?'

'But where will you start?'

'You told me that yourself. There have been two somewhat similar cases in the district.'

'They were in Chedcombe and they weren't exact parallels. The police don't connect them at all. They think they know the girl who's responsible – I told you that – but they haven't any proof. At least, I don't think they have.'

He smiled at her. 'Are you trying to dissuade me?'

'You know I'm not.' She sounded hurt. 'Only I know we'll never get anywhere unless we're quite honest with you.'

'We may not get anywhere anyway,' he warned her. 'But that's where I shall begin, and as you say the police make no connection between the cases no one can object if I talk to Camden about them. Meanwhile—'

'Meanwhile?' Lisa echoed after a moment.

'There's the question of motive. If our client is innocent, and insanity isn't involved—'

'That's the worst thing of all,' said Lisa despairingly. 'There must be dozens of babies in Chedcombe, so why should she come all the way to Madingley to find one? Besides, the others were taken away, not killed on the spot. Only if we rule that out—'

'You can't see who could have had a motive besides Mr Linwood here?'

'He didn't do it!'

'That's the assumption on which we're working. It follows therefore that somebody else did. I've suggested one possibility, but we can't overlook anything. We must also go into the question of who, besides our client, could have had a motive for killing that particular child, Mark Linwood.'

'No one could have a grudge against a two-week-old baby.'

Maitland's eyes met Linwood's, and they exchanged a look of

39

humorous resignation. 'Lisa, dear, you're dithering,' said Oliver frankly. 'If you won't accept this poor deranged girl who is operating in Chedcombe—'

'On whom you seemed quite keen yesterday,' Antony added.

'—I'm afraid you either have to accept my guilt or the fact that someone else has a motive. It isn't likely there are two lunatics going round the district smothering babies, but if you think for a minute you'll see it's quite possible that somebody had a grudge against Sandra.'

'Yes, of course. I'm sorry, Oliver; I'm sorry, Mr Maitland, I'm just being stupid. I think it's because I've been concentrating so hard on Oliver's point of view that the rest of it has seemed to be in the abstract up to now, and it suddenly came home to me exactly what had happened. I don't know too much about Sandra, but if somebody had a grudge against her or against Walter . . . it seems so terrible that it should have been taken out on the baby.'

'At the moment we must just forget that side of it and think of the possibility,' said Maitland firmly. 'You can help me, Mr Linwood. For instance, how long had your cousin been married?'

'A couple of years. Almost exactly a couple of years when he died, because I remember it was June, but I'd have to look it up to give you the exact date.'

'Did you go to the wedding?'

'No. Walter asked me, of course, but it was rather a back-handed sort of invitation really. He said being family I obviously wouldn't want a formal one, but went on to make it quite clear that it would be a very exclusive affair and he didn't think I'd be very comfortable among his and Sandra's friends.'

'I didn't know that,' said Lisa indignantly. 'How perfectly horrid of him,' she went on, but much more uncertainly. Perhaps she had just remembered that the *de mortuis* injunction now applied to Walter Linwood.

'Not really,' said Oliver. 'After all, he was quite right. He suggested that I might like to take a holiday, and even offered to foot the bill . . . a good excuse, you see, for the fact that his only living relation wasn't present. But I saw no reason to put myself out to that extent, I just went into Chedcombe for the day.'

'Had you met Sandra at that time?'

'As a matter of fact I hadn't, though I knew of her existence. Walter and I never cared for the same things, and he was always extremely conscious of his position in the local hierarchy. He'd never have brought her into the Saracen's Head for a quick one for instance, though we really have a nice clientele there – don't we, Lisa? – and lots of good conversation. It was the same about music. He'd go up to London, and get all dressed up, and go to a concert at the Royal Festival Hall or to the opera at Covent Garden. I haven't the faintest idea whether he enjoyed himself when he got there or not, it was the thing to do. But for me the beauty of the concerts in Chedcombe is that they're things people go to, ordinary people, dressed in ordinary comfortable clothes. I grant you you won't hear Maria Callas there, but there's lots of good stuff if you look for it. I never knew Lisa's friend Miss Langhorne – sle married your uncle, I understand, at just about the same time as Lisa married Dominic – but we missed her from the Choral Society when she left.'

'That's funny,' said Antony smiling. 'The first time I met her on the steps of the Shire Hall in Chedcombe I was immediately distracted by a vision of her in one of those long white nightgown things that choral societies will get themselves up in, bringing good tidings to Zion for all she was worth. She's converted my uncle's drawing-room, which is only used on state occasions anyway, into a music room. You remember the wonderful equipment she had, Lisa. When they do want to use it, which fortunately isn't very often, it's the devil's own job putting everything in place again. But I'm getting away from the point. If you didn't meet Sandra before the wedding, when did you first encounter her?'

'One of the first things Walter did when they came back from their honeymoon was to ask me to dinner. A family affair, just the three of us. No need for me to be embarrassed that way by the company of his elegant friends,' said Oliver without resentment.

'How did Sandra receive you?'

'She didn't rush away screaming at the sight of me if that's what you mean,' said Linwood, 'but I expect Walter had warned her what to expect. After that we met occasionally in the village shop and would exchange polite nothings, but some time during each Christmas season that boring family dinner would be repeated.'

'Did you know she was pregnant? When your cousin died, I mean.'

'Yes, I think it was last January that Walter confided the fact to me with a good deal of pride. Funnily enough it never seemed to enter his head that the baby might be anything but a boy, and for some reason I rather took it for granted that he was right about that. As it turned out he was, of course.'

'When he died did you realise the position . . . that your future depended on whether it was a boy or a girl?'

'Never entered my head.' He paused there, looking at counsel for a moment before he went on. 'That's another of the things nobody's going to believe, isn't it?'

'It takes a bit of swallowing,' Maitland admitted. 'You did know about the entail though?'

'Oh yes, Mother told me all about that, and, as I told you, Lisa explained it to me in more detail. But if I could only make you understand how little I wanted to inherit—'

'We're taking that for granted at the moment . . . remember?'

'Yes, but I can see I'm putting you in a difficult position. Did you really mean it when you said you might take my case on? It would please Lisa no end, and I'll absolve you in advance from any responsibility for these further inquiries she has in mind if you like.'

'If Lisa still wants me I'll accept the brief,' said Maitland. 'But I'm afraid, you know, there's no question of my absolving myself, as you put it. It'll have to be all or nothing.'

'That's exactly what I want,' said Lisa. 'You know that.'

'We'll talk about it later,' said Maitland non-committally. 'Am I to take it then, Mr Linwood, that you know very little about Walter and Sandra's friends?'

'I thought it was their enemies you were interested in.'

'So I am. But someone with a grudge of the proportions we are talking about must be someone who knew them well. Was your cousin interested in business in any way?'

'No.'

'Did he run the estate himself?'

'Yes, he did, and oversaw the running of the home farm too.'

'You can probably tell me this, Lisa. Was he a good landlord?'

'Dominic never had any cause to complain. Though I'm not at all sure how Walter would have behaved if any particular piece of land wasn't being farmed well.'

'Have you anybody in mind?'

'No, but Dominic might be able to help you there. I can't see that it would constitute a motive though.'

Maitland was silent for a moment. Then, 'I think you must both resign yourselves to the fact,' he said, 'that if we're to get Oliver out of this mess we have to try everything, however unlikely.' He turned back to Linwood again. 'About their friends and acquaintances,' he repeated, making the words a question.

'There was some name-dropping at those dinners I spoke of,' said Oliver. 'I'm afraid I didn't take much notice and can't remember anybody they sounded particularly intimate with.'

'I shall just have to consult Dominic about that too,' said Antony resignedly. 'Just one more question. What was Walter Linwood's state of health at the time he married?'

'Perfectly normal as far as I know. In fact he always seemed to me rather painfully energetic. It was only after he died that people began to talk about the weakness in his heart when he was a baby.'

'Had you heard anything of it before?'

'No, though I expect my mother knew all about it, as my father certainly must have done. After he died – my father I mean – she may have got the idea there was some inherited weakness, in which case she wouldn't want to mention it to me. In case I worried myself into a decline, you know.'

'That sounds to me very unlikely. You seem to be taking all this very calmly, for instance.'

'What's the point of doing anything else? I'd rather be at home, of course, and naturally I miss my friends, but I don't ask too much out of life. I've got a roof over my head, adequate meals, even though they are rather dull. The library's hopelessly out of date, besides being full of blood and thunder, which seems to me odd. One would think something more elevating . . . however, the chaplain's been very good, getting me things I want to read.' He paused and smiled at Lisa. 'I'm not quite sure whether he considers me a brand to be snatched from the burning, or whether he believes I'm the victim of injustice. In the long run I don't suppose it matters much either way.'

'It won't be for long,' said Lisa passionately, getting to her feet. The two men followed her example.

'As to that,' said Oliver, 'I'm not so sure, and I think if you ask our friend here he'll agree with me. Don't you?' he challenged, turning to Antony.

'Give me a chance to look into things, there's a good chap.'

'You don't need to be tactful with me, you know.'

'I'm not trying to be. I think you realise for yourself the strength of the case against you, and I shouldn't be doing you any favour by trying to minimise that. But Lisa and I haven't even started work yet. Who knows what may turn up?'

II

After Oliver Linwood had been taken back to his cell Lisa was silent until they reached the car, negotiated the rather narrow archway out of the prison courtyard, and were on their way back towards Chedcombe. Then she said, 'You see now – don't you? – that I was right about Oliver.'

'He certainly made visiting a client in prison more easy than I have ever known it. But I'm afraid the best I can do at the moment is to say I have an open mind,' Antony told her.

'But you promised—'

'Yes.' He twisted round in his seat to face her. 'I'll try to be frank with you,' he said. 'I think I should probably have done so in any case because I'm beginning to share your doubt as to Oliver's guilt.'

'I haven't any doubts!'

'No, that was badly phrased. But for myself it's the most that I can say. What I'm trying to tell you is that I'm not quite sure whether I've agreed to what you want for our client's sake or for yours.'

'I don't understand what you mean.'

'I think you're even more concerned about this case than you've told me. And if you'll forgive me for saying so, Lisa, I'd have to be blind and deaf not to detect a certain inconsistency in your attitude. Last night you were all for persuading me that that unfortunate girl in Chedcombe was guilty of this murder as well. Today you were full of arguments against that idea.'

He thought at first that she wasn't going to answer him. The silence had lengthened perceptibly before she said in a small voice, 'They say that some women do act strangely when they're pregnant.'

'Are you telling me—?'

'That I shall be having a baby myself some time in January.'

'My dear child, that's splendid. Aren't you pleased about it?'

'Of course I am, and Dominic's in transports. Only, three babies now . . . murdered. I think I got frightened.' For the first time she took her eyes from the road, though only for a moment, to glance at her companion. 'It was perfectly true, everything I've told you about Oliver, and I'd have wanted your help for him in any case. But being so sure he's innocent I sort of felt the three deaths must be connected, and if you could prove who's doing it, which the police don't seem to be able to do, we should be all right.'

'But only this morning you were saying . . . you were bringing up all sorts of arguments against this girl's guilt.'

'I thought if I tried too hard to persuade you that would be the quickest way of turning you against the idea.'

'I see,' said Antony rather thoughtfully. 'Well, you needn't worry. I mean to look into the matter, but as I said before I've an open mind about whether the Chedcombe deaths and the one in Madingley are connected.'

'I suppose that's the best I can hope for at the moment.'

'I think it is. Where are you taking me now?'

'To the place where I usually have lunch. Dominic promised to meet us there, and you can ask him all those questions that neither Oliver nor I could answer.'

As they went into the restaurant Maitland – who was blessed with a good appetite – looked around him with approval. Not a tea-shoppy kind of place, which immediately raised Lisa even higher in his estimation. Women on their own, in his experience, were only too apt to go in for a dainty type of snack, not enough to keep body and soul together.

Dominic was waiting for them and had obtained a table

strategically placed in a corner where they could survey the whole room. 'Well?' he asked, almost before they could seat themselves.

'He's taking the case,' said Lisa, translating this question accurately, 'but I don't think he's quite sure yet whether Oliver really is innocent.'

'That will come,' said Dominic placidly. 'After all, if you haven't had the opportunity of observing Oliver through the years his philosophy does sound a little strange. Even you, Lisa . . . don't you remember how odd you thought him when you first met?'

'Yes, I did,' she acknowledged. 'I thought it was just a pose, pretending you don't want something you can't have anyway. But it isn't, you know,' she added turning to Maitland. 'He really doesn't care at all about material things.'

'Unfortunately the prosecution will be primed with exact details of his financial position. I think perhaps I ought to have a look at this cottage of his. Do you have the key?'

'Yes, he gave it to me when he was arrested.' Lisa pulled a face. 'You won't like what you see there,' she promised.

'I gathered as much, but it's very necessary to know the worst.'

'I don't mean it's dirty,' she assured him quickly. 'Except, of course, it's bound to have got a bit dusty by now. But he's never made any concessions to his personal comfort.'

'Let me worry about that. There's also his bank manager, you'll have to get a letter of authority from him about that.'

'I very much doubt if he has one.'

'I thought he had a small amount of money invested on your advice, Dominic.'

'Yes, but not in stocks and shares. I couldn't watch him every minute, and I certainly couldn't trust him to deal with that sort of thing himself. So I made him buy an annuity. The income's miserably small, but it's sent directly to him every month.'

'I see. Well, at least that simplifies matters. I suppose you'll tell me he hasn't had a solicitor either, until now.'

'He's never needed one, I think, except to handle the sale of his mother's house and the purchase of the cottage. Your father looked after those things for him, didn't he, Lisa?'

'I'm not really sure.' She did a little mental arithmetic. 'If he did it must have been just before I qualified and joined the practice.'

'Well, we can talk to your father, just in case. I suppose the solicitor for the Linwood estate, whoever he is, is out of bounds now because he'll be giving evidence for the prosecution.'

'Yes, that's so. I've got a copy of his statement, of course. You know all about the entails so I needn't go into that, but the only thing that's really relevant is that he wrote to Oliver after little Mark's death but never got any reply from him. I was hoping, of course, that Oliver had written to him from prison about what could be done for Sandra in the circumstances, even if he's acquitted I know he means to look after her, but I suppose it would have been too sensible to expect him to do that.'

'I doubt if it would have done any good. In court it would just have sounded a piece of insincerity designed to make a good impression.' He paused a moment in case either of his companions had any comment to make, and then went on, 'We can't talk to anybody at Linwood House either, because Sandra and the housemaid you spoke of and the nurse will be giving evidence, I suppose, as all of them were there at the time the baby died and can tell the court about Oliver's visit.'

Lisa nodded. 'All of them, naturally,' she said.

'Is there anything in their statements that I should know about?'

'Hilda says no more than that she let him in, and showed him into the drawing-room. She told Sandra, who came down to join him immediately. When she opened the front door Oliver was standing on the doorstep. There was nothing to suggest that he'd just come along the terrace from where the pram was parked, but that doesn't help us because naturally there wouldn't have been. After the bell rang she had to come from the back of the house to answer it, but another thing about Oliver is that he never wastes energy. He wouldn't be pacing up and down, which might have given her a wrong impression.'

Antony smiled at her. 'Am I supposed to be grateful for that?' he asked. 'What about the nurse, Dora Tompkins did you say her name was?'

'She didn't see him at all until she rushed in after she found the baby dead. She'd helped Sandra dress, by which I imagine she meant she'd got out the things that Sandra wanted to wear, and then stayed in the bedroom tidying up after her. As for Sandra, she said she was surprised to see Oliver, because he'd been to

Walter's funeral and said all the right things, and she couldn't imagine what he wanted unless it was to borrow money. His manner was very strange, almost embarrassed, so she was quite sure that was the reason he'd come. But Oliver didn't know her very well and what he knew I don't think he liked, and he would be embarrassed at trying to make his feelings about her baby being a boy clear to her. I'm sure he'd feel it would be difficult to make her believe he was really pleased.'

'Yes, I can well believe that. Tell me about Sandra. Did you know her before her marriage, Dominic?'

'Only as one does a local girl several years one's junior. That is to say I knew she existed and I saw her at the local hops sometimes. We're a very democratic society, everyone goes.'

'Except Oliver,' Lisa murmured.

'Yes, except Oliver. She was one of those girls who are rather plain and uninteresting really, then suddenly she blossomed out into a raving beauty, and no one was surprised when she got engaged to Walter. He was far the best catch in the district.'

'That sounds rather as if—'

'As if I didn't like the lady. That's true. I said she's beautiful, but there's a hardness about her. I'm sure Walter wasn't distasteful to her, but I very much doubt if she was in love with him as . . . as Lisa and I understand it for instance,' he added rather shamefacedly.

'I see. Have you anything to add to that, Lisa?'

'Not a thing. I only knew Sandra for a couple of years before she married Walter, but I think Dominic's quite right in what he says. She may have been in love with Walter, but I doubt if she'd have married him if he hadn't had money.'

'All right then, tell me about Walter,' Maitland invited. Again the question was addressed to Dominic.

'If you want to know if there was any love between him and Oliver I have to tell you there wasn't. But I don't think there was any malice either, certainly not on Oliver's side. It was just that they were so very unlike.'

'Yes, I can understand that.'

'We saw a good deal of each other in our younger days, before Walter and Oliver went away to school. After that not so much. To go back a little, I've got to say Walter's father, Mark Linwood, was a good landlord, but my father always said he knew which side his bread was buttered, and that it wouldn't pay him to let the property go down. I have to admit though that if a place wasn't being run properly he'd have the tenant out p.d.q., but I don't know that I blame him for that and it hasn't arisen lately. Walter was still at university when his parents were killed, but he was far more interested in the estate than in taking a degree so he came home right away and took over. I don't . . . well I didn't know him well since we grew up, he seemed a bit of a sobersides to me, but I don't know that I've any right to say that. Certainly we were both very sorry when he died so early, it seemed particularly tragic after two years of married life and it was hard to know whether to be glad or sorry that the baby was on the way.'

'Do you mean because of your friendship with Oliver?'

'No, the legal implications never struck me, though Oliver had told me once that none of the family money would ever come his way. Even Lisa didn't know anything about the entail until she got mixed up in Oliver's defence. I meant it might have been a great comfort to Sandra, but she didn't strike me as a maternal type somehow.'

'People's attitudes about that are apt to change when the child is their own,' said Lisa. 'I didn't know you had so much of the feline in you, Dominic.'

'They say it's good for a marriage for both husband and wife to keep a few surprises up their sleeve,' Dominic said rather smugly. 'But seriously, we've dragged Mr Maitland down here and he's been kind enough to say he'll do his best for Oliver. I think we owe him the truth . . . as near as anyone can ever get to it.'

'There speaks a wise man,' said Antony lightly. 'Now what about Walter's and Sandra's friends?'

'They lived rather – rather formally,' said Dominic slowly, as though he found it difficult to find the right words. 'I have to go back to Mark again, Walter's father. He and his wife – she was called Maude if that's any help – entertained all the local bigwigs ceremoniously once or twice a year, or perhaps even oftener if they were more intimate. Even as a bachelor Walter followed the same tradition, inviting his parents' friends and any of their families who were more or less of his own age. After he married Sandra I think the older people dropped out of the picture, they would be on visiting terms with married couples of their own generation. But I don't quite see . . . why do you want to know all this?'

'Because in the case of a baby the motives are very limited. Infanticide isn't unknown by any means, but it's hard to see the lady you've described as being in the state of mind to kill her own child, particularly as that automatically disinherited him and deprived her of her home and income.'

'Infanticide, darling,' said Lisa, seeing her husband looking a little puzzled, 'is legally the killing of a child under the age of twelve months by its own mother.'

'Oh, I see. Well I think you're quite right, we can leave Sandra out of this.'

'Then of course there is the insane killer, and I gather there have been two cases in Chedcombe that may come under this heading.'

'Perhaps not insanity in the legal sense of the word,' said Lisa. 'I mean if the girl were mad she'd be put in an asylum, wouldn't she?'

'Not necessarily. The police have a suspect, from what you told me, who may be deranged on this one point only, but against whom they have no proof whatever. It will certainly have to be looked into, if for no other reason than the possibility of confusing the jury, but there's one other possibility that mustn't be ignored.'

'Revenge,' said Lisa. 'Mr Maitland thinks,' she explained to her husband, 'that someone might have hated Sandra, or even Walter, so much that they killed the child to get back at them.'

'It sounds far-fetched,' said Antony, 'but we can't afford to ignore any possibility, however remote. Because there is still another motive we are at the moment carefully ignoring and that is the financial one. A lot of nonsense is talked about there being no legal necessity to prove a reason for murder. It might be true, though I doubt it, if the entire jury consisted of people bred to the law, but twelve men and women drawn from the general population . . . give them something they can get their teeth into, and you have to admit that a financial motive is more easily understood than almost any other.'

'He means we're in trouble,' said Lisa. Dominic smiled at her.

'Yes, my clever wife, I had understood so much,' he said. 'The trouble is I don't think I can help you,' he added to Maitland.

50

'Neither Walter nor Sandra were people to arouse any very violent emotions, not the sort of thing you're talking about that might give rise to murder.'

'They must have had some more intimate friends than those you spoke of.'

'Yes, I suppose they must, but I don't know them.'

'Some disappointed boyfriend of Sandra's perhaps?'

'One who had borne a grudge for two years? It doesn't sound very likely but I can't help you there either.'

'Then we shall just have to do the work that's nearest. Can either of you think of anyone else I ought to see who hasn't been mentioned so far?'

'Not really, unless . . . you said you wanted to know every detail of Oliver's financial position.'

'I think it's very important.'

'Well there's Martin Weatherby, the editor of the local paper. He's a good friend of Oliver's as well as of ours, and the person responsible for giving him the reviewing jobs for the paper. I think from things he's let drop from time to time that he'd have been only too glad to have given him regular employment. I don't mean reporting, that would have been far too energetic for Oliver to contemplate. But a weekly column perhaps. Mightn't it help to be able to show that some extra income from a source like that would have been available to Oliver if he'd needed it?'

'That sounds a good idea.' To himself Antony was thinking that perhaps Mr Weatherby might be able to give him a slightly less biased opinion of his client. 'Let's make a plan of campaign then.'

'You'll find Martin at the Saracen's Head this evening,' said Lisa. 'At the office he's always frantically busy, and anyway he'll be more relaxed and ready to talk to you after a drink or two.' (So she had guessed part of his reason for wanting that particular conversation, Maitland thought, amused.) 'I think . . . do you want to see Dad?'

'It seems like a good idea.'

'Then we'll go straight to the office when we leave here. After that we'll go back to Madingley and have a look at Oliver's cottage, since you seem to think that's important. You'd better bring a toothbrush with you and stay the night with us. Mrs Biggins, my daily, will have left us a casserole or something . . .

dull but nourishing, and always enough for an army. After that we'll go round to the Saracen's Head, I think you may find it interesting. And tomorrow I'll bring you back into Chedcombe and . . . you say you wanted to see those other people who've lost their babies.'

'I'm afraid I do, and I'll go alone if you'd rather because I don't imagine it will be terribly hilarious. There's also the girl, I think you called her Henrietta Vaughan.'

'Yes. Well, Saturday will be best for all those visits, because there's a chance you'll find them at home. And if you can take it I can,' said Lisa, suddenly looking very determined. 'After all, Oliver is our friend and it's my fault you're getting let in for all this.'

'That sounds an excellent programme,' said Maitland, amused again at her sudden decisiveness. 'And when I go back to the hotel for that toothbrush you spoke of I'll take the opportunity of phoning my wife and telling her I won't be home till Sunday at the earliest, and maybe not even then if anything else turns up.'

III

Ralph Williams was a man who obviously took his profession seriously. Without any change in his attire or his expression he could have gone on stage and been immediately recognised by the audience as the quintessential family solicitor. In conversation, however, he turned out to be a jovial person with an obvious pride in Lisa's accomplishments. 'Not that I agree with her about that rather odd young man, Mr Maitland,' he confided, 'but it will be good experience for her and we don't get too much of that kind of thing around here. To tell you the truth I'm glad enough about that, so if anything does turn up among our clients in the criminal line she'll be very welcome to take it over.'

Antony was thinking that for so small a town, Chedcombe, to his certain knowledge, seemed to have had at least its fair share of dire happenings. Perhaps it showed in his face, or perhaps Williams was a thought reader. The solicitor leaned forward and said confidentially, 'Yes, I've heard of your involvement in various cases here and in Northdean. I'm glad to meet you, as a matter of fact . . . as curious as the next man, and there's been a good deal of talk.' Again Maitland's expression must have betrayed him. 'Well, well, you don't like to think about that I see, but my friend Fred Byron thinks very highly of you and has spoken about you more than once.'

'That's very kind of him.' A little stiffness had come into Antony's tone and Lisa gave him an anxious look. 'I don't think I need keep you long, Mr Williams, it's just that I wondered if there's anything you can tell me about Oliver Linwood, as I understand you acted for him on a couple of occasions. And while we're talking, Lisa,' he added, turning to the girl, 'could you put through a phone call to Inspector Camden – no, I must remember it's Chief Inspector now, isn't it? – and see if you can arrange a meeting. We could see him when we leave here, or tomorrow at his convenience.'

Lisa got up immediately, but then she hesitated. 'And if he asks me what you want to talk to him about?' she said. 'What am I to say to that?'

'I think you'll find that once he knows I'm here he'll be as anxious to see me as I am to see him,' Maitland told her. 'But you can say, if it's absolutely necessary, that I shan't commit the impropriety of trying to talk to him about the Linwood case. I take it he's dealing with the other one too, the Chedcombe children.'

'Yes, he is. Well, I'll do my best,' said Lisa, and went out closing the door behind her. Antony turned to his host.

'A good girl that,' he said warmly, 'and one with a head on her shoulders. You must have been glad when she decided to follow in your footsteps. The law isn't to everyone's taste.'

'No, but I can't take any credit for that. My wife and I adopted her when she was a baby. Didn't she tell you?'

'No, but from the way she spoke of you I don't imagine it's a thing she ever gives a thought to.'

Williams seemed to be following another train of thought. 'I gather you've been to the prison to see Oliver Linwood,' he said. 'What did you make of him?'

'An odd, likeable chap.'

'Yes,' said Williams rather doubtfully. 'All the same I'm

surprised you decided to take the case. You realise, I'm sure, that Lisa isn't quite old enough yet to have realised that even her best friends don't always behave exactly as they should.'

'If we're talking about going around smothering babies that's a very delicate way of putting it,' said Antony, 'but I'll tell you this much – I've told it to Lisa herself – I'm not sure whether I took the case on because of some doubt about Linwood's guilt, or whether it was her persuasion that turned the scale.'

'Or Vera Langhorne's. Lady Harding's I should say, but old habits die hard. She's your aunt by marriage now, I believe.'

'It was Vera's suggestion that I come down here, but she knew that once I had done so I'd make up my own mind whether to accept the brief. I hadn't thought of that though, I suppose you've known Vera for ever.'

'We'd both lived all our lives in Chedcombe until she married and left, and being in more or less the same line of business naturally we came across each other quite often. My wife, Mary, has always been very fond of her and that's how Lisa knows her so well. Anyway, Mr Maitland, for better or worse you've taken on Oliver Linwood's defence. What was it you wanted me to tell you?'

'Anything you know about him that might help in his defence.'

'I did the conveyancing for him as vendor when he sold a house that had belonged to his mother, and again when he bought that hovel he lives in. Also, at Dominic Traherne's instigation, I saw to the purchase of an annuity . . . that was good advice, he'd have probably starved to death by now without it. I didn't know Dominic myself at that time though I'd known his father, which I suppose was why he brought his friend to me.'

'Was that when Lisa and Dominic met?'

'No, Lisa was completing her articles at the time with my agent in London.' He smiled as though some thought amused him. 'That was seven years ago, Mr Maitland, and if you knew Lisa better you'd realise that a three-year engagement wouldn't have been on the cards. When they did get to know each other they were married within a month or two.'

'Lisa tells me Linwood didn't have a bank account. Can you give me details of this annuity, which seems to be his only regular source of income?'

'I can, but not offhand. It's some time ago, and goodness knows where the papers have got to now. But I'll look it up for you, I'll certainly do that.'

'Did you ever have any dealings with the other members of the Linwood family?'

'No, but of course I know of them, and Lisa and Dominic have spoken of them sometimes. I don't even know . . . wait a minute. It could be Fred Byron who deals with their affairs. A good deal of the work he and his late partner took on was among the local landowners . . . as you know yourself, Mr Maitland.'

'For my sins,' said Antony, and hoped the lightness of his tone disguised the fact that he found the memory unpleasant. 'He married Nell Randall, didn't he?'

'Yes, and I've got to say it's turned out very well in spite of the difference in their ages. Would it help if I phoned him and found out—?'

'Not really. Whoever the solicitor for the estate is Lisa has his statement, and though I know Fred Byron would be helpful if he's the man concerned there's no question of my talking to him, because he's being called by the prosecution.'

'Yes, of course, he's bound to be. You see how rusty I am about this kind of thing, Mr Maitland, and how glad I am that Lisa's here to take some of it off my shoulders. But I'm afraid she and Dominic are really concerned about this friend of theirs, and whether she's right about his innocence or not I think they have cause to be.'

'I think so too. I wish I didn't.' And at that moment Lisa came back into the room with the information that she had succeeded in tracking Chief Inspector Camden down, and got his grudging agreement to see Mr Maitland at nine-thirty the following morning at the police station.

'Though I don't think he was really reluctant,' she added. 'There was a sort of the-Lord-hath-delivered-mine-enemy-into-my-hands tone in his voice. Do you know what I mean?'

'I know exactly what you mean,' said Maitland getting to his feet, 'and I shouldn't be surprised if we both enjoyed the interview immensely. But now we've kept your father quite long enough, Lisa. He's going to look up the details of Oliver's annuity for us. I don't suppose the information will be the slightest use, unfortunately, but we may as well be as informed as we can.'

After that they made their farewells. Lisa left her car in what was obviously her usual parking spot and they walked back to the George to collect Antony's overnight bag. 'We may as well have tea while we're here,' he said as they went into the hall. 'I shall be a few minutes, because as I told you, I want to phone Jenny, but by the time Henry's coped with your order I daresay I'll be down again without giving it time to get cold.'

IV

Jenny answered the phone on the first ring, which meant she had either been writing letters or actually waiting for his call, and from the breathless way she greeted him he rather thought the latter was the case. 'I'm so glad you called now, Antony,' she said, 'because I shall be having dinner with Uncle Nick and Vera, and Vera said to go down at tea-time.'

'I'd have known where to find you, love.'

'Yes, I know, but I wanted to talk to you,' said Jenny. Her husband forbore to point out that she could have done that in any case, knowing perfectly well what she meant. 'Antony, are you coming home tonight?'

'No, love, not before Sunday at the earliest. Perhaps not even then, but at the moment I can't see anything very useful to do here.'

'But at least that means you've taken the case?'

'I'm afraid it does.'

'I'm so glad,' said Jenny.

'Glad that I'm not coming home just yet?' he asked, teasing her.

'Of course not! It's just that . . . Antony, have you ever known Vera to be really – really perturbed?'

'She was worried enough about that friend of hers, the Matron of the old people's home, the last time she dispatched me to this hell-hole.'

'Yes, but this is different. She doesn't even know the man who's been arrested, only the girl who's acting for him, and she knows as well as we do that nobody can win every case they take on.'

'She's known Lisa Traherne all her life . . . all Lisa's life, I mean. I suppose she just wants to help her.'

'What is she like?'

He didn't pretend to misunderstand her. 'Charming and intelligent and capable of putting up a good fight if pushed hard enough, I should imagine. Also worried sick over this business, which is, to tell you the truth, a little more complicated than either Uncle Nick or Vera told me.'

'Do you mean she's in love with this Oliver – whatever his name is?'

'Nothing of the sort. She's very much in love with her husband, as he is with her. That's obvious to the meanest intelligence . . . which is about my level in matters of the heart.'

'Then—'

'She has reasons of her own for finding the matter upsetting,' he told her.

'You needn't talk in riddles to me, Antony. Vera explained to me exactly what this man is accused of and though I think it's perfectly horrible I'm not going to get upset about it, particularly if you think he didn't do it.'

'I see.' If he sounded thoughtful, it was because he was realising that however well he felt he knew her, Jenny could never cease to surprise him. 'Then I may as well explain Lisa's attitude to you as well as I can. There have been other – other incidents of the same kind in Chedcombe.'

'But surely that makes a perfect defence. Unless they're accusing your client of those incidents, as you call them, too.'

'No, they think they know who's responsible but they can't prove it. I shall know more about it when I talk to the local police.'

'Can you do that?'

'As they don't admit any connection between these deaths and the case I am engaged in, yes, certainly I can talk to them.'

'Well, I still think . . . but why does that upset Lisa particularly?'

'She's quite convinced all the cases are connected, and equally sure that Oliver had nothing to do with them. And as she's expecting her first child in January she'd like everything to be cleared up before it comes along. It's nonsense, of course, because if you know there's any danger you can quite easily take precautions against it, but I daresay it's a bit much to expect her to be completely reasonable in the circumstances.'

'Poor Lisa,' said Jenny. 'Do you suppose Vera knows all about this?'

'Obviously she knows enough to have rattled her badly from what you say, and you know, love, that it isn't like Vera at all.'

'If it was anyone but her I'd say she'd got the jitters,' Jenny told him. There was a pause during which he distinctly heard her sigh. 'Being fond of people does complicate things, doesn't it?' she said. 'I suppose Vera's afraid that if the matter isn't cleared up Lisa might be upset enough about it to have a miscarriage or something like that.' (For a moment Antony could see her as clearly as if they were in the room together, her chin cocked a little defiantly because she was speaking of a very sensitive subject.)

'If you get the chance you can tell her from me that's nonsense,' he said as bracingly as he could. 'But apart from that there isn't much you *can* tell her except that I'm taking the brief and will do what I can.'

'Perhaps you ought to tell her that yourself on Sunday.'

'Perhaps I shall. Jenny love, are you all right?'

'Missing you, that's all. But I'm glad you're taking the case,' said Jenny firmly, 'because Vera after all . . . she's rather special, isn't she?'

V

When he got down to the lounge the tea had just arrived. Lisa asked him how he liked it and added as she poured, 'Did Mrs Maitland mind very much your not going home tonight?'

'Unfortunately she's had to get used to my rather erratic comings and goings.'

Lisa passed him his cup. 'You didn't tell me, could Dad help you?'

'Except in the matter of the annuity which I mentioned to you, no. He didn't know who the solicitor for the Linwood estate is, but as you've seen his statement I expect you do. Your father thought it might be Mr Byron.'

'Yes, it is. Of course, you know him, don't you?'

'I've had dealings with him on a number of occasions. On the whole I'm glad of that, he won't try to make matters sound worse than they are when we get into court.'

'No, but . . . I know as well as you do that the bare bones of truth are damning enough.'

'We'll have to see what we can do about that. I gather Vera at least will be glad to know I'm staying.' He didn't look at her as he spoke, because the remark was prompted purely by the curiosity that Jenny's statement had aroused in him, but he raised his eyes quickly when she answered enthusiastically.

'She's a darling, isn't she. I hope you didn't mind terribly when she married your uncle.'

'It was a blessing.'

'You sound as if you meant that.'

'I do. And Jenny would tell you the same thing.'

'Do you remember her cottage here?'

'Very well, both before and after it was burned. She was – and still is for that matter – very good at guessing exactly what music would suit her visitor's mood.'

'It was she who taught me to love music,' said Lisa. 'And later when I got older . . . Dad was always very careful not to try to influence me in any way in my choice of profession, he's a much more sensitive man than you might suppose just meeting him casually, and once they'd explained to me I was adopted he was always terrified I might feel grateful. Which I do of course, but when you love people very much that really doesn't enter into it, and after all I've been with them since I was a baby, it's just exactly as if they were my real parents.'

'Of course it is.'

She went on as though he hadn't spoken. 'So when I began to get interested in law it was Vera's books I borrowed. And when I told Dad I wanted him to give me my articles I was able to convince him I really knew what I was talking about and wasn't just doing it to please him.' She paused and then added with an almost complete reversal of subject, 'Vera tells me you don't like

59

Chedcombe, Mr Maitland.'

'I've had one or two cases here that were rather ... distressing,' he admitted.

'Then you know exactly how I feel about Oliver,' she said triumphantly. 'Quite apart from all that nonsense I was talking to you this morning, I mean, after we left the prison. I'm not really a hysterical sort of female, so if you can see your way not to tell Dominic—'

'Unless I'm very much mistaken he knows already,' said Antony, smiling at her.

'But I don't want him to worry about me!'

'What else are husbands for?' he asked lightly. 'To share things with, of course. But if he really doesn't know you needn't worry, my lips are sealed.'

They left the hotel together in perfect amity some ten minutes later. The first part of the journey was familiar to him, but they were soon on strange ground. The Northdean road had obviously been widened at some fairly recent date, but once they took the turning where the signpost said MADINGLEY 3, they were in the sort of lane where if they had met anything larger than a bicycle one or other of the vehicles would certainly have had to back up to the nearest passing point. A number of these wider spaces had been made, not particularly close together, but today all was well and they made the journey without incident.

'This is Madingley,' said Lisa, with a note of pride in her voice, as the road widened again to become a street with houses and shops on either side. 'And that's our cottage, the second on the left. It's quite old,' (which Antony could see for himself) 'and of course there wasn't a garage but there's plenty of room so Dominic had one built when we were married. We thought two cars would be a bit of an extravagance, so he uses one of the vans from the farm, only he thought the neighbours might not like that standing out in the open so it goes into the building and this car of mine stands outside. Not that I really think anyone would have minded in the least, it's not that kind of place. And there's the police station, so Mrs Biggins doesn't have very far to come to work. She's the local constable's wife, I didn't tell you but I daresay you guessed after what Oliver said about Joe. And the Saracen's Head is a little bit further on on the other side, we'll see

60

the sign in a minute, it's perfectly ghastly. And just beyond it there's the lane that leads up to the church and the row of cottages at the other side of the turning is where Oliver lived.'

It was certainly a pleasant village, and quiet too, being so far off the main road. Maitland was doing his best to follow Lisa's rather breathless commentary and at the same time take in the main landmarks. 'And where is Linwood House?' he asked.

'It's just round the next bend, not far at all. We can hardly go up and gape at the scene of the crime, but I'll turn round there, so at least you'll get a glimpse of the house.'

Which was true enough, though not very informative. 'Is Sandra still living there?' asked Antony when the manoeuvre had been performed.

'Yes, I suppose it's the obvious thing, because if Oliver's convicted he can't inherit. What would the position be then?'

'A perfectly horrible mess,' said Maitland frankly, 'and very profitable for Fred Byron I should say. Seriously though, I can't tell you without looking up precedents. If there are any,' he added doubtfully.

'It will be far the best thing if we can get Oliver off,' said Lisa briskly, pulling the car to a standstill outside the third of the row of cottages she had mentioned. She made no immediate attempt, however, to get out. 'Except perhaps for Oliver', she added doubtfully.

'You're not really telling me he'd prefer to be in prison than to have the job of managing the estate.'

'No. Sandra could go on living at Linwood House, but it wouldn't be much fun for her alone, would it? And I'm quite sure there's no law against Oliver giving her an allowance. He'd have to get an agent, of course, and if you could be quite sure the man was honest and wouldn't keep bothering him with questions that might not work out too badly. And perhaps,' she added, and here the doubtful note was even more noticeable, 'I might be able to persuade him to have something done to the cottage. A bathroom and a proper kitchen sink would be something, and a little paint on the woodwork outside. The ones that have been done up are really quite nice.'

Of the seven cottages five had obviously been restored, the only one that matched Oliver's in shabbiness being at the far end of the row, nearest the lane that led up to the church. Lisa sat for a moment contemplating the one they had come to look at and then said briskly, 'Well, you may as well know the worst,' and got out of the car without troubling to look whether another one was coming into whose path she might be stepping. Which might be all right in a place like Madingley, Maitland thought, getting out onto the narrow pavement, but as a man who spent most of his time in London it quite made his flesh creep.

However no harm was done. Lisa came round the car, produced a key with admirable efficiency and without the scrabbling that usually goes on when a woman has to find something in her handbag. 'I warned you it would be dusty,' she said, unlocking the door, 'but that doesn't mean—'

'Any place that's been shut up even for a couple of days begins to look neglected,' Antony assured her. And this was certainly true, but the predicted dust was hardly noticeable. Even the high street in Madingley is not particularly heavily travelled. 'You're right about one thing though,' said Antony, standing and surveying the room into which the front door opened directly. 'Linwood hasn't much idea of making himself comfortable, has he?'

'I warned you about that,' said Lisa again, 'and in a way I think it proves that what we've been telling you is true. He just doesn't care. I mean, even about money . . . I've told him again and again if he had to sell the stuff that belonged to his mother he could at least have kept one chair that was comfortable, and a comfortable bed. But he said he'd rather have the money for other things. The bus fare into Chedcombe when he wants to go there, or a pint at the Saracen's Head when he wants someone to talk to. Dominic said to leave him alone, everyone has to choose his own priorities. Of course he's known Oliver all his life, so this wasn't such a shock to him as it was to me when I first saw it.'

Maitland had taken a few steps into the room and was looking around him with interest. 'I can quite understand how you felt,' he said, but he sounded abstracted and clearly his attention was no longer on his companion. There was a fireplace which still retained last year's ashes, though the hearth had been swept quite neatly. The one ornament was a picture on the mantelshelf in a tarnished silver frame.

'His mother, Millicent Linwood,' Lisa explained, seeing him eyeing it. 'Of course, I never knew her, but Dominic says she was a very nice person.'

'I wonder what she made of her son. After all he was – what was it? – twenty-one or two I suppose when she died.'

'Dominic says—' She broke off and smiled at him. 'I'm not really forever quoting my husband,' she told him, 'but in this case, where he knows the people in the village so well and I'm a comparative newcomer, it just can't be helped.'

'Of course not. What does Dominic say?'

'That she hoped he'd follow in his father's footsteps into the medical profession, and even after he flatly refused to let his Uncle Mark pay for his training she still thought he'd find some job and make a name for himself. He did do some freelance work for the paper until she died, just to provide for his needs and make sure he wasn't making things more difficult for her. I'm sure she must have realised before very long that he was never going to be a nine to five man or anything approaching that.'

'Did Dominic say whether she minded very much?'

'No, he says she was a woman who took things very much as they came. I think he said "placid", only that does sound rather like a cow.'

'I've known cows—' Maitland started, but his eyes had already wandered from the picture and he didn't seem to realise that he'd left the sentence incomplete. There were three chairs arranged round the fireplace, which couldn't by any stretch of the imagination have been called easy but which offered as much in the way of relaxation as anyone could apparently expect in that room. One was an old-fashioned nursing chair, covered in what had once obviously been an attractive brocade, but now with the stuffing emerging in several places. The other two Antony described to himself as modern, but when he came to think of it afterwards it was only too obvious that they had seen many years of service. Both had wooden arms and low hard backs and beside one of them was a standard lamp with a torn shade, and a wooden crate doing service as a table with an untidy pile of newspapers and a book from the County Library lying open but face downwards on top of them.

'I'd better take that back,' said Lisa. 'Unless it's one he got

63

when they were selling them off cheap. He does that sometimes. There are some paperbacks over there but I don't think he really likes them. They get so messy when you keep re-reading them.'

'What is the book?' asked Antony idly.

Lisa picked it up. 'Yes, it does belong to the library,' she said. 'It's a book about China actually. Do you think if the police saw it they'd say it proves he really had a desire for foreign travel?'

Maitland took it from her. 'There are plenty of people who prefer armchair travel to the real kind,' he said. 'In any case this is mainly politics. I don't think it could be said to prove anything either way. Where did he work?'

Lisa smiled again. 'That's a funny word to hear applied to Oliver,' she said. 'That big kitchen table over by the window. You can buy one that size for practically nothing nowadays, since everyone has taken to having kitchens that are more like ships' galleys. There's only one chair' (it was a hard-backed kitchen one) 'but he said it was easily moved about and he used one end to eat his meals on, and you can see there's a typewriter at the other.'

'Yes, I could hardly miss that.' It was an enormous, battered machine with a carriage capable of taking brief paper. 'It's practically an antique,' Antony commented. 'Where on earth did he get it?'

'I found it in the back of a cupboard at the office,' said Lisa. 'Nobody seemed to know it was there, so I got Dad to give it to me.'

It was Maitland's turn to smile. 'A subtle encouragement to the poor chap to work a little harder,' he suggested. 'Did he ever use it?'

'When the spirit moved him,' said Lisa. 'There's some paper in the drawer but he never left it lying about between reviews. He said it might give a false impression.'

That was really all there was to be seen about the living-room, except that it had a flagged floor and a rag rug in front of the hearth that had probably been left there by the previous occupant. 'The kitchen's through here,' said Lisa invitingly, indicating a door at the back of the room. But I don't know about you, I find it even less friendly than this one.'

This was certainly true. It was a warm day, but the kitchen

had a chill about it. 'There was a gas stove in it when Oliver bought the place,' said Lisa, and Antony added mentally, Dominic told me. 'The original range had been taken out but it was probably frightfully inconvenient anyway. But Oliver said all he needed was a couple of gas rings so he sold that too – the gas stove, I mean – though I shouldn't think it fetched very much.'

Oliver Linwood's domestic arrangements seemed to have consisted mainly of a frying pan and a tin kettle, though there was a shelf with some pieces of crockery on it and Lisa opened a drawer in the built-in dresser to show a small collection of aged cutlery. There was a round tin basin in the old-fashioned stone sink and a single tap above it. 'Did he have hot water?' Antony asked.

'Only when he boiled a kettle. He said he managed quite well. In the winter he had that oil stove thing in here for heat. All his toilet things have gone with him, of course. He certainly didn't have any spares.'

'And the lavatory at the bottom of the garden?'

'There isn't a garden, just a square sort of yard, and actually the lavatory is immediately on your right when you open the back door so he always maintained it wasn't any bother at all.'

'Hardy sort of chap. Where did he store his food?'

'There's a bread bin,' said Lisa. 'And the cupboard under the window is draughty so he used to keep things like butter and milk there, and meat too when he bought any. If you look you'll see one of those old-fashioned things for keeping flies off it. But he asked me to get rid of anything that might go bad so I did. The tinned stuff's still there but . . . oh dear, I wonder if he'll ever need it.'

'From the looks of this place,' said Maitland rather grimly, 'I should think prison will make a nice change, practically a holiday. Are there any further shocks for me upstairs?'

'It's no better, but I don't think it's any worse either,' said Lisa. And this proved to be true enough. The small back room over the kitchen wasn't furnished at all, though it had a collection of things of the sort that people usually put in their attics. The front room had a single bed, a table with a lamp, a chest of drawers, and a wardrobe. All had obviously been bought second-hand. 'He said he really didn't need the wardrobe,' Lisa confided, 'a piece of curtain on a rod across one corner would have done just as well. But the man at the shop practically begged him to take it, no one has room for that kind of thing now. So there it is.'

Maitland took one last look round. 'I think,' he said firmly, 'it's high time we went back to your place, since you've been kind enough to invite me. I never thought of myself as being particularly sybaritic, but – good lord! – the desert fathers would have found this a bit thick.'

'Did it do any good your coming here?' asked Lisa as she locked the door behind them.

'I think so. It's a matter of interpretation, after all. The prosecution will have their ideas of how Linwood felt about the way he lived, and I shall do my best to put a completely different aspect on it. The trouble is, I don't know that I understand your friend Oliver at all myself.'

Mrs Biggins' offering turned out to be shepherd's pie, not the casserole Lisa had expected, and a reasonably flavoursome one too. Dominic had arrived home before them and judging from the sound of splashing and a rather tuneless singing that wafted down the stairs towards them was engaged in bathing away the effects of his day's labours. The cottage, which Maitland learned was known locally merely as Traherne's, turned out to be as pleasant indoors as out, though the picturesque effect had not been carried so far as to detract from its comfort. After Oliver Linwood's cottage the effect was one of almost sinful luxury, and Antony sank thankfully into the embraces of a really easy chair. Dominic joined them almost immediately, offered and poured drinks, and while the shepherd's pie was heating demanded and received a comprehensive account of their doings that afternoon. 'My father-in-law, of course, is quite convinced that Oliver's guilty,' he said, when Antony and Lisa had finished telling him in chorus of their visit to the cottage in Church Row. 'And as he isn't a man given to making rash judgements, I'm afraid we must take his opinion as pretty typical. I only hope the sight of Oliver's home didn't give you the wrong impression of him.'

'I think mainly I was puzzled,' Antony admitted. 'And I shall have to work out pretty carefully what I'm going to say in court. All the same I'm glad we went, and grateful to Lisa for taking me.

I hope it may be possible to invent a fairly convincing explanation of the sort of man Linwood must be to have been willing to live like that. He's intelligent after all, the local newspaper was willing to give him a good deal more work than he was ready to do, apparently. With very little effort he could have lived a good deal more comfortably.'

'Yes, that's true. I expect we all got into the habit of accepting him as he is and didn't think too much about it until what happened forced us to.' Dominic dismissed the subject then, perhaps realising that nothing further useful could be said about it for the moment, or maybe feeling that their visitor by now must be heartily sick of it. They talked of many things, and Antony began to feel more relaxed than he had done since he left home. It wasn't until they'd finished their meal that Dominic reverted to Oliver Linwood's affairs again, and then with good reason. 'How are we going to play it this evening?' he asked.

'You're expecting Mr – Weatherby, isn't it? – to be at the pub.'

'I shall be very much surprised if he isn't. Most of our entertaining at home is done at the weekend, by which I mean Saturday and Sunday, when everyone, except hardworking farmers like me, is free to make preparations. But it's liable to be pretty crowded, you're hardly likely to want to talk to him there.'

'No, I thought about that. If you could ask him to leave with us a little early and come back here—'

'And until then you'll remain incognito, we just introduce you as a friend?'

'The latter certainly. I'd like to sit quietly for a while, just listening to any comments I may hear about the affair. It must have caused a pretty good sensation here, and it's hardly likely the subject won't come up sooner or later. But as far as Mr Weatherby is concerned—'

'Do you know him?'

'No, I don't, but I'm very much afraid he may know me. Neither the local nor the national newspapers were exactly silent about the cases I was involved in here . . . in Chedcombe that is, and in Northdean. They'll probably have printed a photograph, but whether he recognises me or not he'll certainly recognise my name.'

'Yes, I suppose so, I hadn't thought of that. But Martin's very discreet. I'll just tell him you'd like to talk to him a little later in the evening and I'm sure he'll get the idea.'

'That sounds splendid. And then about tomorrow . . . I was thinking, Lisa, there's really no need for you to come with me. It's all very informal, and unless we decide to make an issue of the matter in court nothing really to do with us. And I'm sure you could find something better to do with your time.'

She eyed him speculatively for a moment. 'You mean you think it will be very unpleasant and you'd rather spare me,' she said. 'But you're doing us a favour as well as Oliver, and if I can be of any help at all—'

'You can't,' he said bluntly and she smiled.

'I can't say I'm altogether sorry about that. You can have the car if you like,' she offered, 'and then come back here for a council of war after you've finished.'

'That's good of you, but I don't drive.' As usual when he spoke of the disability that prevented him from doing so comfortably a slight stiffness came into his manner. 'If you'd drop me at the police station, and then perhaps leave my bag at the hotel, it will be probably easiest for me to take a series of cabs from then on. I only know Chedcombe superficially, but a taxi driver's knowledge would be useful.'

'I could wait and ferry you around,' she offered.

'And make me feel nervous because I was keeping you waiting. No, I think my way's better, Lisa. And you and Dominic can come in and have dinner with me, and we'll have that discussion you spoke of.'

'All right, but I think you'd better come here again. It will be much more private, and you may just as well leave your things here and stay over again.'

'If that's the way you want it. I expect there's a bus I can take, or perhaps the cabs don't mind coming out as far as this.'

'We'll come and fetch you,' she said firmly. 'And now that's settled, let's get along to the Saracen's Head before they start wondering where we've got to.'

VI

Outside the Saracen's Head had undergone none of the indignities of modernisation, except a little re-pointing a few years before, which had probably been very necessary. The sign was certainly not a thing of beauty, but on closer inspection not as bad as Lisa had intimated. It would be interesting to know exactly how old it was. The paint had faded, the surface was well veined with cracks, and if the artist had intended to convey a sinister impression he had done so only too well. Inside it was just the same, no refurbishing to spoil the character of the place, no attempt at an olde worlde atmosphere; just a few flattish cushions intended to take away some of the hardness of the chairs, and a brass footrail, certainly not original, which from its brightness must surely be somebody's pride and joy.

Once inside Lisa led the way to what was obviously their usual table while Dominic went straight up to the bar. To Maitland's discomfort their entrance was greeted by a short silence before the general greeting that the Trahernes gave the people already there was echoed from all sides. The man already sitting at the table Lisa was making for got up as they approached, a medium-sized man with very dark hair – what was left of it – and equally dark, beetling eyebrows. They were certainly the most obvious thing about him, without them Antony thought it would have been difficult to describe him at all. 'This is Martin Weatherby we were telling you about,' Lisa was saying. 'Mr Maitland, Martin. He'd like to talk to you a bit later, but not here, so perhaps you could come to the cottage with us if we leave a bit early.'

'That would be a pleasure,' said Weatherby, and sounded as though he meant it. 'Will it offend you, Mr Maitland, if I say it's interesting to meet you after reading and writing so much about you over the years. I've seen you in court, of course, but that's hardly the same thing.'

'As a matter of fact I think you might,' said Lisa. 'Offend him,

I mean. I don't think he likes being a celebrity at all.'

'I shouldn't be surprised if he doesn't like newspaper men either,' said Weatherby, more shrewdly than Maitland would have expected. They were all seated again by this time. 'However, needs must when the devil drives . . . isn't that so, Mr Maitland? If I can help you at all I will, of course, and promise not to treat our talk as an interview.'

Dominic had returned by now. 'I brought you a refill, Martin,' he said, putting the tray down and distributing its bounty. 'Has Lisa explained to you—'

'Yes I have, darling, practically in your own words,' said Lisa. 'And if you're going to ask me whether he understood, I should say that he understood only too well.'

Dominic looked from one to the other of them, a little puzzlement showing in his face. 'Well, that must all be for later,' he said, 'only I'm afraid, Antony, if you were expecting some interesting comments from people who've no idea who you are you're out of luck. I said at the bar we'd brought a friend who was staying with us, but they all know exactly who you are and why you're here.'

'I suppose in a country district it would be too much to expect anything else,' said Maitland, rather ruefully. Dominic and Lisa had lapsed into a less formal mode of address over dinner, and for that at least he was glad. 'Was that what they were talking about when we came in . . . Oliver Linwood's arrest?'

'Yes, I suppose so. I mean, quite frankly, nothing else has been talked of in Madingley ever since.'

'Will they go on talking about it now?'

'Of course they will,' said Weatherby, 'they can't keep off the subject. But . . . quite honestly, Mr Maitland, I think I can help you as much as anyone. They've all been telling me what they think, just out of helpfulness, or perhaps hoping to get their name in the paper. And if I may make a suggestion, it might pay you to talk to Ruth and Tom Jenkins. That's the landlord and his wife. Oliver sometimes had a snack here, you'll have gathered he was pretty hard up and you won't find better value than a pub lunch. They both had a soft spot for him I think, and quite often asked him to join them for their evening meal.'

'That's a good idea. They're busy tonight, I can tell that, but

70

perhaps on Sunday morning—'

'I'll arrange it,' Dominic offered. 'Meanwhile, if we sit here quietly – do you mind, Martin? – you'll probably get a pretty good idea of how the village thinks about the whole affair.'

Things didn't quite turn out as they expected. True, after a while the talk did turn back to the murder, though not until a good many curious glances had been cast in Maitland's direction, and all he heard went to confirm Lisa's and Dominic's opinion: the people who frequented the pub at least, if not the rest of the villagers, were unanimously of the opinion that a mistake had been made. Some blamed the police not being able to see beyond the end of their noses (if it had been left to Joe Biggins now things would have gone differently); others thought that though Oliver couldn't have done such a thing he had only himself to blame being misunderstood by strangers.

'Not conducting himself like a Christian,' a man with a ferocious squint remarked, which started a fierce but extremely uninformed argument about the desert fathers – an odd coincidence considering Antony's comment on leaving the cottage in Church Row – and the practical advantages and disadvantages of living the life of a hermit. This was squashed eventually by the landlord, who pointed out that Oliver had never displayed any particular tendencies in this direction. 'Or he wouldn't be so well known to all of us,' he concluded, looking round triumphantly.

'Only trouble is, how's anyone to prove he didn't do it,' said a short, stout lady who hadn't previously spoken. She was wearing a man's cloth cap which she had chosen to put on backwards, and darted a sharp, inquisitive look at Antony as she spoke.

'That poor girl in Chedcombe's the guilty party it stands to reason,' said the man who had spoken disparagingly of Oliver's lifestyle. 'Anything can happen in a big place like that, begging your pardon, Mrs Traherne.'

Lisa only smiled at him and shook her head. Martin Weatherby said suddenly, 'If it was her, how did she get here?'

'The bus—' someone suggested.

'Surely rather a public means of transport if she had murder in mind.'

'Well we all know she wasn't all there. Besides, she could have

71

walked, couldn't she?'

'Certainly. But that raises another question. Did anybody see her here?'

'Wouldn't know her if we saw her, would we? There's been talk, but no pictures in the papers. And if that's Oliver's lawyer from London,' the man with the squint added rather belligerently, 'why doesn't he ask his own questions?'

Weatherby turned to Maitland with a rather apologetic smile. 'I was trying to be helpful,' he said. 'But the floor's yours if you want to take it.'

'All right.' If he disliked the turn events were taking he made no sign. 'The girl you're talking about—'

'Henrietta Vaughan,' Lisa prompted him quietly.

'Yes, Mrs Vaughan.'

To his surprise that was greeted with a shout of laughter, mainly from the male members of his audience. But it was a rather sour-faced woman who spoke. 'If she's married I never heard it,' she announced. 'An unmarried mother, that's what they call them. Lucky to lose her baby if you ask me.'

'You sound as if you knew her, madam.'

'Not me. Only by reputation.'

'You're implying it's a bad one. I understand she lost her baby recently. Has she any other children?'

'Not that I ever heard. And it was only after the other babies started disappearing and then turning up dead that the rumours started getting about. Couldn't stand it, you see, losing the kid, so she took it out on those as had them. And husbands too,' she added righteously.

'I see.' If her attitude aroused any distaste in him he gave no sign. 'And though you'd heard of her none of you knew this girl by sight?' he added slowly, looked round at the assembly. There were about twenty people present, but only three women besides Lisa, and the general murmur of assent was unmistakable.

'Then the next question's obvious. Did any of you see a stranger about on the day the Linwood baby was killed?'

'If we had we'd have said so fast enough,' said the man who had first brought up the subject of police inefficiency. 'And if anyone in the village had seen anything suspicious Mrs Croft at the shop would have heard of it. Wouldn't you, missus?'

'Nothing like that,' said the third woman, who might have been the twin of the lady in the cloth cap except that she was rather more conventionally attired. 'If they had I'd have sent them round to Joe Biggins double quick, you can be sure of that.' Antony found it only too easy to believe her, though he couldn't quite make up his mind whether the regret in her voice was for Oliver's predicament, or for the fact that she had lost what might be the only chance in her life of getting into the limelight.

'It's always been my experience,' he said, 'that nothing went on in the country – nothing as unusual as seeing a stranger about for instance – without someone or other observing it. I haven't always lived in London, you know,' he added, seeing a look of incredulity on some of his hearers' faces. 'Look how quickly you guessed my identity.'

'That wasn't difficult, you being with Mrs Traherne and all.'

'Perhaps not. Anyway, let's grant for the sake of argument that this poor girl had become deranged by her own child's death, and was responsible for what happened to the two babies in Chedcombe. It's a small place,' he went on, forgetting for the moment that one of his audience at least regarded it as a large town, 'but there must be plenty of babies being born there. Why should she come to Madingley?'

'That's easy! If you weren't on the watch in Chedcombe now you'd be a fool, there'll be no babies left about there unattended. And if you're going to ask how she knew of the Linwood kid,' continued the belligerent man, who in spite of his expressed sympathy for Oliver seemed to resent Maitland's questions, 'it was in the paper, wasn't it? Not just the births column either, there was a bit I remember about Walter Linwood's tragic death, and then the baby being born just two weeks later.'

'Two weeks and two days,' the woman in the cloth cap corrected him. 'And that's all nonsense anyway. I'm not saying what might or might not have happened in Chedcombe' (her tone implied that the five miles between village and town put the latter into another world) 'but that Sandra was a flirt. Always was, even when she was a dumpy little girl. Naming no names but you'll find someone had an eye on her, and didn't want to be bothered with the kid.'

That silenced Maitland for a moment, and this time it was

Dominic who stepped into the breach. 'But killing little Mark cut off a considerable source of income,' he pointed out. 'Even supposing you were right, don't you think it would have been worth while looking after the child in order to keep the money?'

'We all know about that silly business now,' said the woman in the cloth cap, with a look at Antony rather as though she suspected that the law had been of his making. 'But that wasn't until after Oliver was arrested. A rich widow, that's what we thought Sandra was.'

'And so she should have been,' said the belligerent man, 'in any properly ordered society.'

There were some murmurs of 'That's right,' but on the whole the feeling of the company seemed to be in favour of – or perhaps it should be said against – the unfortunate Henrietta Vaughan.

Maitland thought it was time to call it a day. He drained his glass, glanced quickly round the table and noted that his companions had all finished their drinks, and got up purposefully. 'It's been very interesting,' he said politely by way of farewell to the group they were leaving behind them. 'I was afraid we'd be getting into the realms of slander at any moment,' he added as the four of them set off down the empty street towards the Trahernes' cottage. Nothing more was said until they were safely indoors with the curtains drawn and the lamps lighted. The windows were open back and front, making the room pleasantly cool after the heat of the day. 'But I think we'd better close the ones onto the street,' said Maitland. 'We don't want to be overheard.'

'You're beginning to intrigue me,' said Martin Weatherby. 'I gather you're regarding me in the nature of a witness.' He was obviously quite familiar with the layout, and was already making his way down the room to where the chairs were arranged round the window that looked over the garden.

'And also trusting in your discretion,' said Antony following him. 'Which Lisa and Dominic tell me I may do.'

'That's asking rather a lot of a newspaper man,' said Weatherby smiling at him. 'You know, the gossip among the representatives of the national press when you were here before was that you didn't care for the members of our profession.'

'I don't much care for publicity,' said Maitland, hoping that the evasiveness of the reply would pass unnoticed.

'Well, I won't promise not to have a reporter at the trial when it comes on, but anything that's said between these four walls is off the record, as I told you earlier,' Martin promised.

'Thank you, that's good enough for me. Do you have any opinion about this business?'

'I share the general feeling in the village about Oliver's innocence,' said Weatherby. 'But that's hardly helpful.'

'Except that it surprises me a little. That it should be so unanimous, I mean.'

'They can't believe that anything so unpleasant as child murder could be the responsibility of one of their own people.'

'*And things are done you'd not believe at Madingley on Christmas Eve,*' Maitland murmured.

'Yes, but that was Madingley in Cambridgeshire, wasn't it? That, in the villagers' opinion, would be something quite different. If they'd ever heard of Rupert Brooke, of course.'

Lisa and Dominic had joined them by now. 'They weren't *quite* unanimous about the murderer coming from outside the village,' Dominic remarked.

'You mean the lady who thought Sandra Linwood might have had a secret lover? At least I suppose that's what she meant. She had a point about the man in the street not understanding the law of entail, but is there anybody in the village who might fit that description?'

'I'm not quite sure about Sandra being a flirt before her marriage,' said Martin Weatherby slowly, 'though I think she probably was. What I am sure about is that she was a snob, there'd be no "Lady Chatterley's lover" about it. I suppose I might be said to fit the bill as I've been a widower for nearly ten years, though I imagine if she thought about me at all it was as someone of her father's generation.'

'Don't be silly, Martin,' said Lisa.

Weatherby smiled at her but otherwise took no notice of the remark. 'I can give you one pretty good argument against that secret lover theory though,' he said.

'That Walter and Sandra had only been married for about two years,' said Antony.

'And I thought all lawyers were cynical! Seriously, I just don't know the answer to that . . . to what Sandra felt about her husband, I mean, though I think she was in love with him. But if she had been carrying on with someone else, if you'll forgive that rather old-fashioned way of putting it, she would certainly have told him the way things were left. Admittedly, she'd have had nothing of her own after young Mark came of age, but that was looking a long time into the future, and it was hardly likely he'd leave her unprovided for even then.'

'Let's leave the possibility of love and marriage out of it then. What do you know about Henrietta Vaughan?'

'Nothing much, except that she had a baby boy who was born dead, on the thirteenth of June last. And, of course, I'd never even heard of her until the rumours began to get about that the police suspected her of kidnapping and killing two local children.'

'That's been puzzling me. How *did* the rumours get about? I can't believe the police were quite so indiscreet.'

'The fact that they interviewed her would be quite sufficient.'

'But why did they interview her in the first place?'

'Henrietta's next door neighbour went to them with the story that she'd been behaving strangely.'

'Any details about that?'

'No, I'm afraid not.'

'At least you know this other woman's name?'

'Marilyn Parker. I expect Lisa has Miss Vaughan's address, and as I said, Mrs Parker lives next door.'

'Do you believe this theory?'

'The police haven't been able to prove anything, at least not so far as I've heard.'

'That doesn't answer my question. I gather the idea is that her own child's death temporarily unhinged her, wouldn't that have been evidence? Wouldn't that have been a reason for committing her to an asylum?'

'It's not so easily done,' said Lisa. 'And if she was a little mad this was perhaps the only way it showed itself . . . I've always heard it said that completely motiveless murders are the hardest of all to solve.'

'If Miss Vaughan committed them they wouldn't exactly have been motiveless,' Antony pointed out. 'But I see what you mean all the same. And Mr Weatherby still hasn't answered my

76

question, what he thinks of the theory.'

'The trouble is I can't think of any other,' said Martin. 'But that's hardly a satisfactory basis for bringing an accusation, as you very well know. However, if you insist on an answer I suppose I should say I think it's possible, even probable, that the girl is responsible for what happened in Chedcombe. But whether she came to Linwood House and found Mark Linwood asleep in his pram at precisely the moment he was left alone is quite another matter.'

'The police at least seem to have found no difficulty in believing in two murderers.'

'They're obsessed with Oliver's motive, which you must admit is a good one. Or would be, if anyone else was concerned.'

'Well the possibility of a connection will have to be looked into,' said Maitland, not sounding as though he relished the idea. 'Another thing I wanted to ask you, Mr Weatherby, is whether you know anything at all about Walter and Sandra Linwood's friends. Offhand, I find it difficult to believe that the baby was killed out of spite towards his mother. Surely that would have resulted in Sandra's murder, not his. But to cover every possibility—'

'You're asking about their *friends*, Mr Maitland,' said Martin, stressing the word. 'Surely—'

'If someone had a grudge it must be someone they knew well,' said Antony, concealing well enough his weariness at having to make this particular explanation yet again. 'I don't suppose he or she went around wearing a placard declaring their true feelings, or even let them show. But it's just occurred to me, if it was a revenge killing—'

'Well?' asked all his hearers in unison when he let the sentence trail into silence.

'It might not have been such a bad idea after all. I don't know Sandra Linwood, but to deprive her of her baby and her livelihood at one fell swoop . . . which would she have minded more, Lisa?'

'I'll answer that,' said Dominic. 'We've told you she wasn't the maternal type. I'm sure she grieved very sincerely for young Mark, any mother would. But the loss of a fortune would be a more lasting sorrow.'

'Yes, I see.'

'I have to say I agree with that,' said Martin Weatherby. 'But you were asking about their circle, who may have been friends or enemies in disguise. I'm pretty sure they knew everybody who was anybody in the county, but not intimately. The people they were closest to, and met with most often, were Charles and Jean Martin, who live on the outskirts of Northdean. He has a few directorships in the City, and goes up to town occasionally, but mostly they're at home. I can't give you their address offhand, but they're in the phone book. The other close friend is Cliff Elliott, who lives in Chedcombe and is the administrator at St Luke's hospital there. He's a doctor himself, by the way. I know him quite well, a good sort of man, a widower like myself, but still in his late thirties, or forty at the most.'

'And you can't think of anybody else?' Weatherby shook his head. 'Or of any reason why one of those people—'

'No reason in the world.' This was said rather quickly. 'And wouldn't it be rather odd if there were two people in the district . . . do you believe in coincidences, Mr Maitland?'

'They happen,' said Antony, who had spent most of his life in wholehearted agreement with the implications of the question, but recently had learned a more cautious approach. 'I think you're saying that if we grant Oliver Linwood's innocence, the person who killed the babies in Chedcombe – Henrietta Vaughan or another – is the only alternative.'

'I thought we were all agreed about Oliver's innocence.'

'For the purpose of my inquiries . . . I have to start somewhere,' said Antony apologetically. 'But I'm very grateful to you, Mr Weatherby, at least these friends of Walter and Sandra Linwood may be able to tell me more about their affairs than you can. So you see you've given me several new lines of inquiry.'

'I'm glad of that,' said Martin, but he didn't sound as if he altogether relished the assurance.

Dominic was on his feet. 'And now we can have the other half,' he said, 'which Antony didn't give us time for at the pub.' And their talk turned to other subjects, but somehow the relaxation that Maitland had felt earlier in the evening had deserted him.

'Well?' demanded Lisa, after Martin Weatherby had left them to retrace his steps to his own cottage.

'It's an odd situation,' said Maitland cautiously. 'If we could go into court with a jury entirely drawn from Madingley people it would be one thing, but does this unanimity extend to Chedcombe?'

'I shouldn't think so. You know how it is,' said Lisa, in a rather despairing tone, 'people are so terribly inclined to think that where there's smoke there's fire. And nobody there really knows Oliver, except I suppose a few people at the newspaper. And we can hardly insist on a jury entirely composed of them either.' She paused, eyeing him rather doubtfully. 'You know,' she said, 'I can't help agreeing with Martin. By far the most likely thing is that all three deaths were the responsibility of the same person.'

'I think so too, but we have to take everything into consideration,' Antony reminded her. 'I'd like to see these other friends of the Linwoods though.'

'We won't have time tomorrow, at least I don't think so.'

'No, I thought perhaps you'd take me to see Dr Elliott, I gather he lives in or near Chedcombe, on Sunday morning if that's convenient for him. That is, if you really mean it about my coming back here tomorrow night.'

'I shall probably die of curiosity if you don't,' said Lisa frankly. 'And most likely Dominic would too.'

'All right then, we'll arrange it that way, or rather I'll leave it to you to arrange it, if you can. Then we could go back and see the Martins — that was the name Mr Weatherby mentioned, wasn't it? — and I could catch the train from Northdean after we've seen them.'

'Well, it's too late to do anything about it now,' said Lisa practically, 'but I'll get on to that tomorrow after I've dropped you off at the police station.'

'That's splendid. And that way you'll both know exactly as much as I do,' said Antony, looking from one to the other of his hosts.

But, as Lisa said to her husband a few minutes later when they were alone together in their bedroom, 'We may know everything he's said and done, but we still shan't know what he thinks.' But the morrow, in one respect at least, was to prove her wrong about that.

Saturday, 19th July

I

Maitland rather expected that he would be kept kicking his heels at the police station for a while the following morning, while Detective Chief Inspector Camden asserted his independence. To his relief however, he was taken immediately in tow by a uniformed constable, and shown to the detective's office. They exchanged rather wary greetings, and Antony took the opportunity of congratulating the other man on his promotion. It was three years, nearer three and a half years, since they had met, and Antony's first thought, bringing back the previous occasions vividly, was that Camden was on the short side for a policeman and that his face looked very much as though it had been carved out of a block of wood by somebody with no great skill in the art. He was very dark of complexion, and not at all given to showing his feelings, except insofar as he was apt to exude a faint air of disapproving of everything and everybody.

'I understand you are undertaking Oliver Linwood's defence,' Camden said, coming to the point immediately. 'As investigating officer I shouldn't need to tell you that I can't discuss the matter.'

'If you thought that's what I've come for I'm surprised you've granted me this interview,' Antony told him. 'My client's young cousin is not the only child who has met a violent end in the district recently.'

'So that's it! The matter is under investigation, Mr Maitland—'

'And you're getting nowhere,' said Antony sympathetically, and surprised a fleeting look of what might have been satisfaction in the other man's eyes, which he decided – for the moment at least – to ignore. 'You won't be surprised, however,' he went on, 'that I'd like to know a little more about these other deaths.'

'If you think you can get evidence about them allowed in court—'

'One can always try,' said Maitland vaguely. He pulled one of his rather ragged envelopes from his pocket and made a show of consulting it. 'I have some notes of the dates here, perhaps you could confirm them for me.'

'Then perhaps you'd better begin with Walter Linwood's death. If he hadn't died, his cousin Oliver would have had no motive for getting rid of the child,' said Camden rather spitefully.

Antony refrained from pointing out that Camden himself had contended that the Madingley affair shouldn't be discussed. 'Very well,' he said equably. 'Walter died on June the ninth last, his son was born on the twenty-fifth of that month, and killed on the eighth of July. But at the moment I'm interested in the deaths that occurred in Chedcombe, which I believe we can properly discuss.'

'There has been enough publicity about them locally.' Camden's tone was stiff. 'I really don't see what more you can want from me.'

'Confirmation, as I said. The first note I have concerns a girl called Henrietta Vaughan whose baby was born dead on the thirteenth of June.'

'Born dead, not murdered.'

'You know what Chedcombe is,' said Maitland. 'You must know even better than I do. Things get about, and I've heard it said that the poor girl has been questioned several times by you or some of your minions with reference to the deaths that followed.'

'I fail to see how that concerns you, Mr Maitland.'

'Well, at least you confirm the date I gave you, the thirteenth of June.'

'As I recall that's quite correct.'

'My next note concerns a rather older child, three months to be exact, Louis, the son of John and Louise Swift of this town. The date I have for his death is exactly a week later, the twentieth of June.'

'That is also correct. And if you will insist on playing out this farce to the end I may as well tell you without further delay that the next death took place only three days later; another boy, Charles, a little younger than the first, the son of Ernest and Caroline Blunt.'

'Thank you, Chief Inspector.' There was no more than a trace of irony in Maitland's voice. 'It's good of you to be so helpful.'

'I'm glad you appreciate it. Now let me give you another piece

81

of information, Mr Maitland, which may have escaped your notice. If you're trying to draw a parallel between the three deaths you're going to be unlucky. There is no doubt in my mind that the two instances you've just referred to were connected, but they bear no comparison to the death of the Linwood baby.'

'Without knowing very much about it I can think of certain resemblances.'

'The Swift baby was left in his pram outside the supermarket nearest his parents' home. When Mrs Swift came out after about ten minutes, baby and pram were gone. Later the pram was found empty, and still later the little boy . . . dead. He had been rather inexpertly hidden under a bush in the local park.'

'And the Blunt child?'

'That too started as kidnapping, and in the same park where Louis Swift's body was found. Mrs Blunt left the pram for only a moment she said, though I should guess it was a little longer, to visit the ladies' room. The park is very heavily used in the summer and there are facilities down by the lake where she'd been sitting taking the sun. This time the baby was found first, in almost the same place as the Swift child had been, and the empty pram only later at the other side of the park.'

'Have you given this information to Mrs Traherne?'

'There was no need. Neither event has any connection with the case against Oliver Linwood. In any event it seems she knew enough herself to tell you about them.'

'And when a similar death occurred in a village not five miles from Chedcombe you made no connection?'

'I've told you there was no reason why we should. In the two cases we've been discussing the children were taken away and only later found dead. I've yet to learn that that is what happened to the Linwood child.'

'I can think of two . . . no, three similarities between the deaths, however.'

'In that case no doubt you will be good enough to inform me of them.'

'I'd be only too happy to do so. Each of the murdered children was a boy, each of them was smothered . . . I'm right about that, aren't I?'

Camden didn't answer that directly. 'And the third similarity?' he asked.

'Why, the dates of course. Each death, and I'm including Henrietta Vaughan's baby here, took place after Walter Linwood died of a heart attack.'

'If you can see any significance in that fact—'

Maitland gave him a sudden, unexpected smile. 'Oh, I can't, Chief Inspector . . . not yet,' he admitted. 'But I'm working on it, you know.'

Camden came to his feet. 'If that's all, Mr Maitland—' He didn't even attempt to complete the sentence.

'Almost all,' said Antony, rising in his turn. 'I should very much like to know what made you suspect the Vaughan girl.'

It was Camden's turn to smile. 'Routine, Mr Maitland, a thing I doubt you'd know very much about,' he said. 'And if I may give you a word of advice—'

'I shall be grateful,' said Antony formally.

'That I take leave to doubt. However, I'll give you my opinion all the same. I shouldn't count too much on the fact that our investigation into the Chedcombe deaths is getting nowhere. So if I were you I should proceed with the preparation of your case on rather more orthodox lines. Or better still, read your brief and act on it, and don't take the matter any further than that.'

'I'm obliged, Chief Inspector.' Antony's tone was cordial. He went to the door, but turned with his hand on the knob. 'Do you happen to know Sir Alfred Godalming?' he asked, and went straight on to answer his own question. 'Of course you do, he was Chief Constable of Westhampton for a while, wasn't he? Before he took over as Assistant Commissioner (Crime) at Scotland Yard. I haven't the pleasure of his acquaintance yet myself, but I can't help feeling that if he were here he'd be in complete agreement with you.'

He went out before Camden could make any response, and the door closed very gently behind him.

II

From the police station it was an easy walk round to the hotel, where Maitland went up to his room for the last time to call Jenny and give her the time of his arrival home the next day.

'Rather later than I'd hoped, love,' he said, 'things keep coming up.'

'Helpful things?' asked Jenny hopefully.

'Not so as you'd notice it. However, I've hardly started yet, so perhaps—'

'If someone's killing babies they ought to be stopped,' she said firmly.

'Even if it's nothing to do with the matter I'm working on?' asked Antony, amused and relieved by her attitude.

'Of course,' said Jenny. Obviously to her the fact was self-evident. 'I know you don't like Chedcombe,' she added severely, 'but that's no reason for allowing the population to be decimated.'

'My dearest love, you've been talking to Uncle Nick.'

'Of course I have, they've been doing their best to see that I'm not lonely,' said Jenny. 'But he's worried about Vera, and she's . . . oh well, she's just worried.'

'If you think back, love, you'll remember she always had a weakness for getting people she believed to be innocent out of trouble. Think of the first time she accosted me, just on the grounds that the accused was a nice girl.'

'But she doesn't even know this Oliver Linwood,' Jenny protested. 'Anyway, Antony, they're coming to dinner with me tomorrow night, so don't eat on the train. I'll make the meal a bit later than usual, then you'll have time for a drink first.'

'And cross-examination by two learned counsel,' said Maitland, not sounding particularly pleased by the prospect. 'However, as there's no way of getting out of it I suppose the sooner we get it over the better. At least the long vacation's coming up, which is a thought to hold on to.'

After he'd rung off he took a quick look round the room to see if he'd left anything, which he hadn't, used the telephone again to call a cab, and went downstairs to check out and pay for the night he had and the night he hadn't spent at the George. By the time he had done this the taxi was waiting. He consulted the list Lisa had given him and gave the driver the Swifts' address.

Talking to the man as he went (a much preferable occupation to thinking about the difficulties of the interviews to come) he discovered that all the addresses for which he was bound were in very much the same area, a suburb of Chedcombe, if so small a town could be regarded as having suburbs, which lay roughly to the north-west. 'I'm not quite sure how long my various errands will take,' he said, 'but if I could hire you for the rest of the day that would be a great convenience. I have to get back to Madingley, probably in the late afternoon, so I shouldn't keep you too late.'

'That's all right.' The prospect of a steady day's employment instead of plying for hire seemed to have a cheering effect on the driver. A few minutes more conversation and the bargain was struck. 'Here we are, number seventeen you said. I'll have to turn round and park on the other side of the street, you'll find me there when you come out.'

It was a semi-detached house, probably no more than ten years old; well-maintained, with a small patch of lawn in front and a flowerbed mainly devoted to roses. Probably there was a larger garden at the back. To his relief, though the garage doors were open there was a car inside. It would have been wiser, he knew, to phone for an appointment, but explaining his rather delicate errand over the telephone would have been more than he could face, certainly more than he would have asked Lisa to undertake in the present circumstances.

But he was in luck. The door was opened by a fair-haired girl who couldn't have been more than twenty. (Or am I reaching the age when everyone looks terribly young?) Maitland introduced himself, the diffident air he could assume at will not exactly an illusion this time. 'If you're Mrs Swift I'd very much like to have a word with your husband and yourself,' he concluded.

'A lawyer? I don't understand. Unless it's about that girl the police were asking us about. Have they made an arrest?'

'No, it's . . . perhaps if I could explain just once to both of you together,' he suggested.

'John's in the garden,' she said. 'We could talk out there as it's such a lovely day. You'd better come through the house, it's the quickest way.'

John Swift was probably a few years older than his wife, a sturdy young man engaged in spraying yet more roses. When Louise had introduced Antony rather breathlessly he gave him a straight look and said as she had done, 'I don't understand.'

'I ought to begin by telling you how very sorry I was to hear of your loss, and I'm sorry too to ask you to cast your minds back to such an unhappy time.'

John Swift shot a quick look at his wife, but though her lips had tightened a little she was listening calmly. 'Have they arrested the person who – who took Louis?' he asked. 'Because if you're acting for her—'

'Nothing like that. Did you read of the death of a child in Madingley?'

'Yes, but that had nothing to do with us. The police had already made an arrest when we first heard of it, and . . . quite frankly I went to the Magistrates' Court here because I wondered . . . but he had a motive for what he did. It couldn't have been anything to do with what happened to Louis.'

'That's what I'm wondering, and why I came to you for help in spite of the fact that I knew I was going to hurt you. I'm acting for Oliver Linwood.'

'He killed his cousin's baby,' said Louise very quietly.

'Forgive me, we don't know that yet. I have very grave doubts about it myself,' said Antony, and only realised as he spoke that he was telling the truth, though the doubts he denied as to Oliver's innocence would almost certainly return to plague him later. 'So you see the fact that there were two somewhat similar cases in the neighbourhood has to be taken into consideration if only in fairness to my client.'

John Swift pondered that for a moment, and then said abruptly, 'Let's sit down,' and led the way to where garden chairs were arranged round a table with a brightly coloured umbrella. 'It's only a month,' he said. 'A month tomorrow, by the date. Louise has been a brick about it, but—'

'Too soon to open the wound,' said Antony. 'Believe me, I can understand that and I wouldn't have dreamed of approaching you if it hadn't been so urgent.'

Perhaps the very genuine distress he felt was more evident to Louise than to her husband. 'I don't mind talking about it,' she said, 'when there's a good reason for it, not just curiosity. You wouldn't believe how tactless people can be, sometimes when they mean to be kind.' Her glance at her husband was pure compassion and perhaps her next words were meant for him.

'We're young,' she said reassuringly. 'I've kept all Louis's things, my sister says that's morbid but we'll need them . . . next time.'

Antony smiled at her though his next words were for John. 'I hope you realise that you've been blessed with a very exceptional wife,' he said. 'Shall we get the worst bit over first? If you'd just tell me what happened—'

'I've had some letters,' said Louise steadily. 'Anonymous letters. Perhaps you can guess the kind of thing.'

'I'm afraid I can. The only thing to do is to put them straight into the fire.'

'I ought to have got rid of them, but the police said they might provide a clue. One of them might be from the person who took him.' They seemed to have agreed on this euphemism, a thing Antony felt he could well understand. 'I don't quite see the reasoning behind that, because whoever it was must have been mad, but that just makes it worse somehow. And I don't blame myself, nobody could have loved Louis more than I did . . . than we did. There's a sort of shopping centre not too far away, and most of the people who go there are our neighbours. It was the most natural thing in the world to leave him in his pram outside the supermarket, I'd done it many times before and usually there'd be someone talking to him when I came out again. I wasn't gone more than a few minutes. It was a Friday, but if you go early there isn't much of a queue at the cash desks. That day was no different, but there were some people about when I found the pram had been moved and I asked everyone I could see. Two people said they'd seen the pram but they hadn't noticed who took it away. So I rushed into the chemist's next door and they let me use the telephone, but I didn't wait for the police to come as they told me to do but I went everywhere I could think of hoping I could find him myself. But it was much later in the day—'

'No need to go into that,' said Antony hastily. 'You said the police had mentioned a girl to you, Mrs Swift. Do you know who it was?'

'Henrietta Vaughan, not that they mentioned her name but people talk, you know.'

'Do you know her?'

'No. She doesn't live very far from here I believe, and they say she had an illegitimate child who was born dead, and it seems to have sent her a little bit mad. I don't know if they're right about her, you know what queer ideas people can get, but I can understand – just – that if she was very upset about losing her own baby a kind of terrible jealousy might have taken hold of her.'

'Then there's only one other thing I have to ask you. Do you know the Linwoods?'

'No. It was terrible for her, Mrs Linwood, wasn't it? First her husband and then her baby. Do you really think that the brother might not have done it?'

'Oliver Linwood was Walter's cousin, not his brother. And I really think . . . you've been kinder to me, both of you, than I perhaps deserve but if it's a question of an innocent man going to prison for a long time . . . I don't like to ask you this, but if we decide to try to confuse the issue by introducing evidence about these cases in Chedcombe would one of you be willing to testify?'

'That had better be me,' said John. 'If it's a matter of justice, of course we can't refuse. He isn't mad is he?' he asked, the question obviously suddenly occurring to him. 'I mean, he couldn't be the one—'

'If there's one thing I'm sure of it's that he had nothing to do with what happened to you,' Antony assured him. 'Do you know the Blunts? I believe they live quite near here.'

'I know her by sight,' Louise volunteered, 'but that's all. I did think about calling on them to offer our sympathy, but then I wondered if it might just make matters worse.'

Maitland was on his feet. 'I think a visit from you would do anybody good,' he said warmly. 'And if you can find it in your heart to forgive me—'

'There's nothing to forgive.' She held out her hand to him. 'John will show you out,' she said. 'I think I'll just sit here quietly for a while.'

They had taken their leave at the front door when a sudden thought struck Antony and he turned to ask, 'By the way, where did Mrs Swift go to have her baby?'

'St Luke's, it has the best maternity ward in Chedcombe.' His expression warmed at a sudden pleasant thought. 'They were all very good to her there, but there was one nurse in particular, a Pakistani, Dera Mohamad, who's called here several times since

– since it happened. I think she's nearly as upset about Louis as we are.'

'Is Dera here in Chedcombe?'

'Yes, do you know her?'

'On and off for a number of years. The last time I saw her she was at an old people's home at the other side of town. You said Dera Mohamad, so I suppose she isn't married yet. Does she live in the nurses' home, do you know?'

'Yes, I think she does.' He was still standing in the doorway when Antony had crossed the road to the waiting car, and raised a hand in salute as it drove off.

Looking back at it in retrospect Maitland couldn't at first decide which had made his task more difficult, the kindness he had received from the Swifts or the very different reception which Ernest and Caroline Blunt had given him. Their house was a much larger one, dating perhaps from the 1920s, detached, and standing in its own grounds. As soon as the car turned into the drive Antony got an immediate impression that the place resented the other smaller dwellings that had grown up around it over the years. Whether he was right about that or not, the idea certainly didn't appear far-fetched after his talk with the occupants.

This time it was Ernest Blunt who came to the door. He received Antony's explanation coldly and only rather grudgingly let him in to talk to his wife as well. 'Not to be wondered at,' he said as they went. 'Whole neighbourhood's going down. If the police don't do something soon we'll none of us be safe in our beds.'

He was a tall man, dressed even on this summer weekend with careful elegance, and as soon as they reached the small sitting-room where Mrs Blunt was to be found, Maitland saw that the two of them made a perfect pair. 'Cooler here than in the drawing-room,' said Ernest, obviously not by way of apology but in order to impress their visitor with the fact that other and better rooms were available when they chose to use them. 'This is Mr Maitland, Carrie. He says he's a lawyer, acting for the man who killed the baby in Madingley. He seems to think we can help him, though I'm blessed if I can see how.'

Antony started on his careful expression of regret, both for

89

their loss and for bringing it again to their minds by this intrusion. Carrie Blunt waved both condolences and apology aside. 'Do they think Oliver Linwood was responsible for what happened to us as well?' she asked.

'On the contrary, the police are quite sure the cases aren't connected in any way. But I do feel, in fairness to my client, that the coincidence should be brought before the court if the judge allows it. That's why I'm here to ask your help.'

'Oliver Linwood's a queer fish,' said Ernest. 'I could believe anything of him myself.'

'You know him then?'

'He's not the sort of person I'd care to have any dealings with. We used to dine with Walter and Sandra though, and we heard a good deal about him from them, one way and another.'

'Poor Sandra,' said Carrie. Antony, who was reproaching himself because his sympathies were not engaged, couldn't help the thought that there was no real feeling behind the remark. 'To lose them both so quickly,' she went on. 'I don't know how you feel about it, Ernest, but I wouldn't lift a finger to help Oliver. Have you seen the way he lived? I've never been inside that dreadful cottage, of course, but he's quite capable of getting a job and living like anybody else. So I'm afraid you've come to the wrong place, Mr Maitland. We have troubles enough of our own.'

It was obvious that either of these two would prove a witness extremely hostile to Oliver's interests. It was hardly worth asking but, 'Can you tell me anything at all about the Linwoods . . . who might have a grudge against them, for instance?' Maitland wondered.

'I can see no reason at all,' said Ernest coldly, 'for looking any further than the man who had an extremely good motive. As for intruding on our grief . . . my wife has been extremely upset.'

There was nothing for Antony to do but suppress the desire to say, she doesn't look it, and take his leave, expressing his regrets once again. It was just one more coincidence that the Blunts had known Walter and Sandra Linwood, though probably not as well as they would have liked to make it sound. As for the murders, Lisa could *subpoena* the investigating officer perhaps, though if it was Camden, as he seemed to remember her telling him, as a witness he wouldn't prove much more favourable to their case. Perhaps the police surgeon, he might be less prejudiced. That was something he must discuss with Lisa tonight.

Meanwhile there was his patient driver, who'd evidently been doing a little brooding of his own over the list of addresses. 'Now I wouldn't have said you looked like police,' he remarked when Antony got in beside him.

Thinking of some of his acquaintances in the force Maitland nearly said, Thank goodness for that anyway. But then he remembered that he had some good friends there too and confined himself to asking, 'What makes you think I might be?'

'These people you've been visiting, there's been lots in the paper about them and what happened to their babies,' the driver explained. 'And this next address. That'll be where the Vaughan girl lives, won't it?'

'Don't tell me her name has been in the newspapers.'

'No, but there's been talk. There's always talk in Chedcombe,' he answered, a thing that Maitland knew only too well. 'So I thought perhaps you were making an investigation into the murders.'

'In a way I am,' Antony told him, 'but not on behalf of the police. Do you know somewhere around here where we could get some lunch? It seems to me about time we refreshed ourselves.'

'As long as you don't mean to get me tiddly, *they* wouldn't like it,' said the driver darkly. 'But a half of bitter wouldn't do much harm, there's a pub round the corner if that'd suit you.'

'It would suit me admirably. I like pubs.' And sure enough this was an excellent specimen, with a plain but good menu, and a first class brand on tap of the drink the driver had chosen. Maitland joined him in that, and managed to steer the talk away from the baby murders for the length of their stay. In a way, he concluded, his talk with the Blunts, though hardly productive, had been less unpleasant than his visit to the more sympathetic Swifts, but there was still Henrietta Vaughan to come, and what he was going to say to her he couldn't think. However, it might not arise immediately. It had perhaps not been too surprising that the couples he had visited that morning were both available. Saturday was probably not the day either of them would choose for shopping, but on a fine weekend afternoon . . . well, there was nothing for it but to go and see.

Their destination was a terraced house, the whole row very neat and well-kept, with clean curtains and well-polished brass knockers. A rather stout, motherly-looking woman came to the door, which alarmed him for a moment as he had learned that appearances can often be deceptive. But when he asked rather tentatively for Miss Vaughan she held the door wide and invited him in with undoubted cordiality. 'Yes, she's in, poor girl,' she said, 'shut up in her room. She lodges with me you know. And since there's been all this talk I can't get her to go out, though a bit of sunshine would do her good. But I'll tell her you're here and you can talk in the parlour.'

'Just a moment. Perhaps I could have a word with you first.'

She'd reached the doorway of the room but now she turned and looked him up and down. 'You look all right to me,' she said, 'but being as she's no one else to look out for her perhaps it'd be as well if you tell me what it's about.'

'Yes, of course,' said Maitland, more willingly than he felt. She turned immediately and led the way into the little room, as neat and clean as the exterior of the house, but crammed with far too much furniture, and with every single space that could possibly hold an ornament of some kind filled. 'You haven't told me your name, Mrs—'

'That was a long time ago,' she said, presumably referring to the married state. 'Everyone calls me Minnie, and that's good enough.' She sat down firmly, and waved him to a chair opposite her, a Victorian chair of extreme discomfort, with pieces of wood in all the wrong places, as he found the moment he sat down. 'Now then!' she said.

This explanation was even more difficult than the one to the Swifts had been, but he managed it at last under Minnie's unswerving stare, which he began to find rather intimidating after a while. 'You're not trying to prove Henrietta Vaughan killed all these children?' she asked him when he had finished. 'I know what people are saying, but it's all lies.'

'I'm not trying to prove anything except the truth. I believe the police are wrong about my client, Oliver Linwood, and I don't much care for coincidences.'

'You mean it's not likely there are two people killing babies in this district?'

'I mean exactly that. But I realise it isn't impossible, so what I'm trying to do is conduct an inquiry on both lines at once. The last thing I want to do is to hurt Miss Vaughan more than she's been hurt already, but I thought if I could just see her I might be able to make up my mind—'

'Whether you should look any further,' she finished the sentence for him. 'Well you should, I can tell you that, but I think you mean well so I'll let you see for yourself.' She started to get up but he stopped her with a gesture.

'You could help me if you would,' he told her. 'Tell me something about Miss Vaughan.'

'She's a good girl,' said Minnie defiantly, 'for all I know she was wrong letting that chap have his way with her.'

'Couldn't we go a bit further back than that?'

'If you want. She's twenty-two years old and I knew her parents, so you may say I've known her since she was born. Her father died in an accident at work, and her mother of cancer two years later. That was four years ago and she's been with me ever since. And paying her way too, until the baby was too near for her to go on working, and when I think of that nice boy Eddie wanting to marry her—'

'You're confusing me, Minnie,' said Maitland, venturing to use her name for the first time. 'Are you telling me Eddie is the father of the child she lost?'

'No, nothing like that. Only they'd been going steady for two years or more, and nothing wrong between them I'll stake my life on that, when this other chap came along and turned her head.'

'Who was he . . . this other chap?'

'A professional man, that impressed her, you see. Not that I thought that much about it myself, a clerk in Mr Byron's office, that's all he was, for all that he qualified two or three years ago.'

'Mr Byron the solicitor?'

'That's right. We all know Mr Byron in Chedcombe, a fine man with a fine reputation, and I'd have gone to him myself when Henrietta confided to me about the baby only she begged me not to. He'd dropped her by then you see and she said, I have my pride. But there's Eddie ready to marry her and would have brought up the child too if it had lived just like one of his own. He's a good boy, and fond of her . . . you wouldn't believe. But first she said she was too ashamed, though I think she'd have got over that if it hadn't been for the rumours starting. You know what it is in a place like this—'

'I do indeed,' said Maitland, with feeling.

'—and there's no way a girl like her can escape from them without going right away. But his job is here and she didn't want to hurt him.'

'Tell me then about the baby, and how its loss affected her.'

'She went to St Luke's, most of them do round here, it's nearest and the people who look after the deliveries know their job. But she was in labour three days, poor child, and then they had to tell her . . . it never even breathed. I was there, of course, and they let me see her, but she didn't even cry, just took my hand and turned her head away to show she didn't want to talk about it. Never a tear she's shed as far as I know from that day to this.'

'And when she came home? How was she then?'

'Not mad, that's what they're saying, isn't it? The shock deranged her,' she quoted with a savage intonation that she hadn't previously employed and that he thought was quite foreign to her nature. 'I'll tell you exactly Mr – Mr Maitland, wasn't it? She was stunned, went about like someone in a dream. She wasn't fit to go back to work at the supermarket where she'd been a cashier—'

'At the shopping centre near here?' Antony interrupted her.

'The same one where the Swift baby disappeared,' said Minnie rather grimly. 'That's one of the things they're saying now makes it look worse, but don't you go getting any wrong ideas into your head. I'd got her helping me, she was always one to make herself useful, and doing the shopping and such like. And the weather was so good, she'd always liked the park so she went there quite a lot. It's as if everything had been arranged, once the story began to spread, to make it look as if she'd really done those things.'

'How did the story get about?'

'That Marilyn next door, a fine friend she turned out to be. That's where this deranged business started and I know for a fact she talked to the local bobby. The police were in to see her before they came to Henrietta the first time.'

'When was this? Before or after the second baby was killed?'

'After. But not until the following week. It was a Saturday I remember.'

'Early in July then. You weren't able to give her an alibi for either of the disappearances?'

'No I wasn't, but even so there was nothing they could prove.'

'Is that when she stopped going out?'

'No, not till she heard the stories, and that was when she was doing the weekend shopping.'

Maitland already had his envelope out for consultation. 'Which day was that?' he inquired.

'Always on a Friday.'

'After Mark Linwood was killed then. That's a pity,' said Antony, whose ever-ready sympathies had already been aroused. 'Tell me, Minnie, *could* she have taken the bus to Madingley on the eighth of July and walked up to Linwood Hall and come home again without you knowing?'

Perhaps she realised already where his feelings were leading him for she answered readily enough. 'That's something I can't do, Mr Maitland. I went out that morning to see my sister at the other side of town, and didn't get home till dinner-time.'

'I see.' The envelope went back into his pocket again. 'I should like to see Miss Vaughan for a moment if I may,' he added, but he knew already that there was no way he could reconcile it with his conscience to involve her in Oliver Linwood's misfortunes. In the short interval between Minnie leaving the room and returning with Henrietta he was wrestling with the problem of whether the fact of the murders might be introduced, without making matters worse for her.

She came in hesitantly, a tall slim girl with straight fair hair and a pallor that was almost frightening. 'Minnie told me why you were here,' she said. 'I'm sorry for the man you're trying to help, I'm sorry for anybody who's falsely accused because I know what it's like, but I know too what it's like to lose your baby, and I couldn't have done anything to deprive another woman of hers.'

Maitland was at her side in a moment and had taken her hand in his. 'Miss Vaughan,' he said, 'I came here because I felt I owed it to my client, and I'm more sorry than I can say if I've upset you, but now I'm glad I did come.'

'Why?' she asked, with all the simplicity of a child, but he was no longer under any doubt, this girl was as sane as he was. And she was gentle, not jealous, or revengeful, or any of the things he had been wondering about.

'Because . . . will you trust me, and tell me what the police said to you?'

'They didn't ask me about Madingley,' she told him. 'That's what you're interested in, isn't it?'

'Yes, I'm not forgetting that, but just for the moment let's concentrate on you.'

'They wanted to know exactly where I was when the Swift baby and the Blunt baby were taken away and then found dead. I've never seen a dead baby, you know, they wouldn't let me see mine, but I don't think the police believed that.'

'Could you tell them where you were?'

'I think I was in the park on both occasions, but – I know it sounds silly – but one place has seemed very like another lately and I don't think I was noticing enough to swear to it.'

'Who came to see you?'

'That Detective Camden,' said Minnie from the background. 'Chief Inspector, he calls himself.'

'I think it's his correct title,' Antony told her absently. 'He had another officer with him, of course.'

'Yes, there were two of them, but I never heard the other fellow's name.'

'How many times did they come?'

'Just the twice, but they said they'd be back. Do you think,' asked Minnie anxiously, 'they could make a case of it?'

'I've a horrible feeling they may try,' said Antony. His eyes were on Henrietta's face but she heard his words with no visible sign of emotion. 'Henrietta, listen to me. If they come again, when they come again, will you be sure not to talk to them except in Minnie's presence.'

'She wouldn't let me do that anyway,' the girl assured him.

'No, but she might be out. Will you promise me—?'

'Yes, of course,' she said readily.

'I haven't quite finished. Even when you're together I don't want another question answered, no statement made, nothing. Do either of you know a solicitor?' The question was out before he thought, and he didn't realise its ineptitude until he saw Henrietta blush. No use recommending Fred Byron, that was certain. 'If it turns out you need advice get in touch with

Williams & Traherne, and ask for Lisa Traherne. I know her and I'll tell her you may be in touch with her.'

'That means you think I'm going to be arrested,' said Henrietta, turning a serious look on him.

'It means . . . it means we've got to be prepared for anything. Henrietta, when I asked you to trust me I didn't necessarily mean I could do anything for you, but I'm going to try.'

'Thank you,' she said gravely. Then she turned to look at Minnie. 'You see I was quite right,' she said, 'refusing to marry Eddie. I couldn't have borne to get him mixed up in all this.'

Maitland's left hand went up, taking her by the shoulder and shaking her gently. 'If you mean what I think you mean that's nonsense,' he said bluntly. 'If you're in love with him tell him so. Anything's better than being shut out by someone you're fond of, that would hurt him more than anything else.'

'You're quite right, I do love him. I knew that long before the baby came even. But don't you see – ?'

'I see you're being very foolish. I told you you could only trust me to try to do something for you, not to succeed, but you can trust me about this. Ring up Eddie, Minnie will do it for you, and talk to him this evening. You'll both feel the better for it.'

This time Henrietta's, 'Thank you' was muffled by her handkerchief. 'That's the first time I've seen her cry,' said Minnie as she saw him out and gave him another of those disconcertingly penetrating looks. 'But I think you mean well so I'll thank you too,' she added, and smiled at him for the first time before she closed the door.

III

Maitland's intention had been to try next to see Henrietta's neighbour, Marilyn Parker, but in view of the decision he had come to and announced loudly and clearly both to Miss Vaughan and her landlady there seemed to be no point in this. If what he had come to fear after his talk with Camden took place she would be one of the prosecution's main witnesses, and it might be easier to cross-examine her effectively in court if there had been no

97

previous encounter. But an idea was forming, still vaguely, at the back of his mind, and he thought as he had some time in hand before Lisa and Dominic would be expecting him back at Madingley he would try to see Dera Mohamad. In any case, he liked the girl, it would be pleasant to get her latest news.

He consulted his patient driver, and discovered that St Luke's Hospital was not very far away. An inquiry at the Nurses' Home provided the information that Sister Mohamad was on duty, and in answer to his further question, still in the maternity ward. In view of her advanced status it seemed quite worth while seeing if she had time to talk to him. Matron, he thought with unconscious cynicism, was not likely to be doing her rounds at this hour on a Saturday afternoon. And sure enough all was quiet, no births apparently imminent, and no complications resulting from the ones that had already taken place. Dera, very trim in her uniform, received him joyously.

'I am being so glad to see you, Mr Maitland,' she told him. 'If you are coming in here we can talk together and the nurses will tell me if I am being needed.' She led the way into a small room, of which his only later recollection was of a rather brilliant whiteness, though this couldn't have been quite correct because there was certainly a desk and chair at which she seated herself with the air of being well accustomed to doing so, and pushed a pile of what he assumed to be patients' records to one side. 'What is it you are wanting?' she asked.

'As usual, Dera, a little information. But that can wait for a moment, tell me about yourself. I thought you were quite settled down in the job you had when I saw you last.'

'This is what I am thinking too, but things change.'

'You mean the things that happened at the nursing-home that was connected to the Restawhile Hotel?'

'Partly that. I am telling you then that I think it is easier to be working in a small place, but St Luke's is not being one of the biggest hospitals, and I find it is good to be working with the babies. Besides—'

'Besides what, Dera?' he prompted her when she hesitated.

'In two or three months' time I am being married.'

'Sister Mohamad, that's the best news I've heard for a long time,' said Antony fervently. 'I hope you'll be very happy, and as

98

for your future husband, he's a lucky man.'

'It is nice of you to be saying so.' Dera sounded serious, but her pleasure was obvious. 'The gentleman he worked for has been so kind, he is helping Paul to be a doctor. I shall stay here until he is finishing his studies, and then we will have a home and babies of our own.'

'That sounds an excellent programme. Tell me about Paul.'

'He is of my own people – that is best I am thinking – but here in England longer than my family. Also he is a Christian and I am learning . . . some things are being difficult, Mr Maitland, but I am thinking that before long all will be well. But you are having some reason for asking to see me. I must not be delaying you in this way.'

'We're old friends, Dera. You know I like to hear that things are going well for you.'

'Yes, I know, but that is not why you are coming.'

He smiled at that. 'You're quite right, of course. I'm engaged in my usual job of asking questions, and it's just possible, considering the nature of the case, that you might be able to help me.'

'The babies?' she asked quickly. 'That is being the most terrible thing I am ever hearing of. Almost the most terrible thing,' she added, so that Antony thought suddenly of her brother who had died, and of the young man who had ended up in prison and whom she had thought – he never knew how seriously – of marrying. But that was many years ago, and Dera, for all her fragile prettiness, lacked nothing in strength of character.

'That's exactly what I mean,' he said. 'I know, for instance, that Mrs John Swift had her baby here.'

'Yes, she is in my ward, such a nice lady. And the baby, a fine boy, not giving us a moment's anxiety. When I am hearing what happened it is almost impossible to believe, but I go of course as soon as I am off duty to see if I am being able to help her.'

'You went to the Swifts' house?' asked Maitland eagerly.

'Yes, of course I am going.' The answer to that question seemed to Dera the most obvious thing in the world. 'We were being good friends, Mrs Swift and I, and though there is nothing anyone can be doing at a time like that, I thought perhaps . . . someone to talk to—'

This was better than he had hoped. 'And were you able to help her that way? Did she talk to you?' he inquired.

'Yes, she was telling me just what had happened. Blaming herself I think, though it would not be occurring to anyone else to do so.' The anonymous letters Louise had received were obviously something beyond her comprehension. 'Her husband, I have met him too, in the hospital, of course, when he was coming to see her and again at their home. I am going there twice again after that first time.'

'Did Mrs Swift tell you exactly what had happened?'

'Yes, I think it is relieving her to talk. But why, Mr Maitland, why do you want to know these things?'

'Because another baby was murdered, in Madingley, five miles away from here. A man is accused whom I do not believe to be guilty, but he is said to have a motive. These other cases might create perhaps a doubt in the mind of the jury.'

'Oh yes, I am seeing that very well. If there is someone mad, and who else would be hurting a little one like that? But there is talk you know—'

'I know, I've heard it. But I've seen the girl, Dera, and I'm convinced she would no more have done such a thing than . . . than you would.'

She looked at him for a long moment. 'Then I must be believing you about that,' she said. 'But I still am not seeing—'

'The police believe the two cases are not connected. What I'm trying to say is, the two murders here in Chedcombe, and the other one in Madingley. They may be right, but whether they are or not I should like if I can to help the girl whom popular gossip is accusing.'

'Then I am telling you, though I do not see what good it is doing. Mrs Swift wheeled little Louis in his pram round to the shopping centre, and left him alone for just a few minutes. No one can be blaming her, until that day everyone is doing that. But then the pram is gone and the police are thinking, she says, that a woman is most likely to have taken it, for who would be thinking anything wrong about that. And then later in the park the empty pram, and later still the dead child.'

'Mr and Mrs Swift have talked to me, and were very kind. But there was a point beyond which I didn't wish to press them. The means of death—?'

'Asphyxiation without doubt.' Again she paused and looked at him. 'You are thinking, Mr Maitland, that in babies this is being difficult to know for certain.'

'You're the expert, Dera, but I have heard of crib deaths.'

'Yes, if he had been found dead in his pram or in his cot then natural disease would have been the first thought in everyone's mind. But you are knowing I am sure that when there must be an autopsy a pathologist is called. This I am not telling Mrs Swift, but there were microscopic inflammatory lesions in both the upper and lower respiratory tracts. Still death might have been natural, if it were not for what had happened.'

This time Antony smiled openly at her. The things she had learned in the course of her profession obviously came under a different heading from everyday chit-chat. 'You've done your homework, Dera,' he commended her. 'The police felt then immediately that this was a case of kidnapping followed by murder?'

'Yes they did, and then when only three days later the same thing is happening to Mrs Blunt's baby . . . how could they be in any doubt?'

'Obviously, Dera, you've heard the pathologist's report discussed.'

'Because I am making quotations? Yes, of course, I am hearing discussions. Tell me, Mr Maitland, the baby in Madingley, was that a boy too?'

'Yes, it was.'

'And dying in the same way?'

'Not taken away from the place where he was sleeping in his pram. But there's no doubt at all that he was suffocated because his pillow had been placed over his face.'

'It is not being quite the same then.'

'No, but the circumstances were a little different. Nobody overlooked the place where the pram had been parked.'

'As always, Mr Maitland, you are having an answer for everything. Is there something else I can tell you?'

'Perhaps, perhaps not. The lady who lost her baby in Madingley had her delivery at home, but was Mrs Ernest Blunt in your care?'

This time it was Dera's usually grave face that showed the flicker of a smile. 'There is a saying I am hearing you use I think, "for my sins". She is not being in the ward, but in a private room, and I am being told off to look after her. This I do not like, she is being a hard lady to please, and I am not thinking that she is much interested in the child.'

'Why did you think that, Dera?'

'They have other children, three others, the youngest already being away at boarding school. She has said to me herself this one was being an accident. I thought her feelings would be changed when he arrived, but so little interest . . . I am being unhappy to see it.'

'Did you visit her too after the murder?'

'Only once. Mr Maitland, I would not be saying these things to anyone but you because you are telling me you need my help. All the right things she says, how terrible, how broken-hearted she is. But I am feeling in my heart that she does not care at all.'

'I see.' He thought about that for a moment. 'And the girl whose baby was born dead, Dera, she too was here at St Luke's?'

'The one they are talking about?' Antony nodded. 'I am not believing what they say and perhaps you will be telling me it is because I have such sorrow for her. To suffer so much, and then . . . nothing!'

'Were you there when she was told?'

'Yes, the doctor is asking me to "stand by" he says, because I am being good friends with Henrietta. She is not crying, but this I am thinking is not her nature. There is a word, two words, that Paul is using when I tell him, but I am not remembering.'

'Perhaps . . . passive acceptance,' Antony hazarded.

'How are you knowing this?'

'I've met Henrietta . . . remember?'

'And you are making your own decision. I am telling you, Mr Maitland, you are right. But because she is not making hysterics people think . . . I am not knowing what they think. That she is not being normal and that her grief will show itself in other ways.'

'Have you visited her at home?'

'Yes, but it is not being easy to find her there. Minnie – you are meeting Minnie?'

'I am indeed. An admirable lady.'

'Yes, so kind. Henrietta likes to walk, she is telling me, or to sit in the park. When sometimes I am finding her at home she is being glad, I think, but just for the company, not for talking. But when the stories are starting, then I am not seeing her. She is refusing to leave her room.'

'But you don't think she's unhinged by her experience?'

'Uh—?'

'Driven mad, mad enough to do what is being said of her.'

'I am thinking you know very well, Mr Maitland, that I am knowing this is not so.'

'Then we are in complete agreement. Dera, if it became necessary, would you repeat what you've told me – just about Henrietta – in a court of law?'

'Paul would be telling me it was my duty.'

Antony chose to take this as agreement. 'Good for Paul!' he said enthusiastically. 'Have any other of your charges lost their babies lately?'

'For some time now we are being very fortunate.'

'No one who might have taken the route Henrietta is supposed to have taken?'

'No one at all.'

He got to his feet. 'I must go now, but I'm very grateful to you, Dera.'

'I am not liking being unkind about Mrs Blunt, but am I being a help to you?'

'To be honest, that's something I can't tell you yet. At the very least though, of great help in sorting things out.' He was on his feet as he spoke. 'Thank you again, and now I'll let you get back to your duties. But don't forget to let me know when the wedding is, I mean to be there if I can.'

IV

So he asked his faithful driver to take him back to Madingley and the Traherne cottage. Lisa, he had a feeling, would protest at the extravagance, though perhaps not very seriously, and she would certainly forget all about it when he disclosed something of the results of his day's activities.

Not having taken the time to interview Marilyn Parker – he had a feeling his temper wouldn't be proof against what he felt would be entirely gratuitous gossip – he was a little earlier than expected. By the time he had paid off his driver and written down his telephone number, just in case, Lisa had already opened the front door, and when he followed her into the hall Dominic, looking quite indecently clean and refreshed, was just coming down the stairs, his hair still wet from the bath which he evidently took at the end of each day's labours. Lisa confined her expostulation to saying, 'I'd have come for you if you'd phoned me,' but Dominic took one look at their visitor and said more practically, 'I don't think it's too early for a drink.'

There was a little argument about whether they should stay indoors or go out, but presently they were seated in the chairs grouped round the window overlooking the garden. A pleasant prospect, and even with the windows wide probably preferable to Dominic, who had almost certainly spent the whole day in the open air. Lisa was obviously itching to question Antony, but had the grace to allow him a little time to settle down. He realised as he sipped his drink that he was desperately tired, and only wished that the discussion could be postponed until he knew a little more. But Lisa had a right to know, more than that there were things she must know, and he broke the silence himself by saying, 'Not an entirely productive day.'

'Did you expect it to be?' said Lisa.

'Not exactly. Not at this stage. But I'd better tell you.' So he gave them an account of his day, starting with the visit to Camden, and going right through until the time he left Dera Mohamad. On that last talk he was inclined to linger, as being the one bright spot he could think of. 'She's a nice girl, and what's more she knows her stuff,' he assured Lisa. 'If you're going to St Luke's—'

'They say it's the best place, so I am.'

'Then you'll get the best of care. I've known her for years—'

Lisa, however, at the moment had her professional hat on, and was not at all inclined to be sidetracked. 'That's all very well,' she said, 'but if you've ruled out this girl, Henrietta Vaughan ... how can you be so sure?'

The question was not unexpected, and he'd already given it a good deal of thought. 'Uncle Nick would say guesswork,' he admitted reluctantly, 'and in a way I suppose he'd be right, though I'd rather call it instinct.' He paused, looking from one to the other of them and then went on, 'I only know that in this case I'm absolutely convinced that she had nothing to do with any of the deaths.'

'Which is more than you can say about Oliver?' said Lisa belligerently.

'Perhaps it is, I don't know. But I can say truthfully that if I had to bet on it, I'd put my money on his innocence too.'

Dominic got up and refilled their glasses. 'Why?' he asked, when Lisa didn't immediately respond.

'Two things, I suppose. Thank you, Dominic, all this talking does make me thirsty. One is that, like you, I can't see him committing any kind of a murder, particularly that of a child, and particularly not for gain. And the other thing is . . . we've talked about coincidences before, but I can't see it as likely there'd be two people in this small area going around smothering infants. Chief Inspector Camden wouldn't believe me, but—'

'Oh him!' said Lisa. 'You mean it's unlikely that Oliver would be the one to do such a thing?'

'Yes, and about that at least I know you agree with me. There's not much use talking the subject to death, Lisa, but a couple of things arise that I think you'd better deal with. The first is that I've got a nasty feeling Camden is going to go the whole way over Henrietta Vaughan.'

'Arrest her, you mean?'

'Yes. From something he said I've a feeling he may have more evidence than we know about. Of course he was quite within his rights not to tell me.'

'You mean something she lied to you about?'

'No, I don't mean that, she was very vague about where she was at the time of both kidnappings, but she thinks she was in the park, which doesn't sound good. But I took your name in vain, Lisa. I told her if the police questioned her again to get in touch with you.'

'But I'm acting for Oliver.'

'You're trying to tell me a conflict of interest might be involved.

If that should prove to be the case, of course, you'd have to withdraw, but the only way really to resolve all this is to find out who the guilty party is, and that, I'm hoping, should exonerate both Oliver and Henrietta.'

'I see,' said Lisa rather faintly, and as clearly as if she had spoken them Antony could sense in her doubts similar to those that had plagued Vera in the early days of their acquaintance.

'You're feeling as though you've got a tiger by the tail,' he said sympathetically.

'Not exactly.' She sounded hesitant, but then she grinned at him. 'Rather as though I'd conjured up the devil,' she said, 'and didn't know how to get rid of him again.'

'You can always withdraw your instructions.'

'I don't want to do that,' she said quickly.

'Even though I may have saddled you with a quite unwanted client?'

'No, because—'

'Don't tell me you believe I mean well.'

'I wasn't going to say that. Only that I think you've some further reason for wanting to help Henrietta Vaughan. As though you . . . as though you felt responsible for her somehow.'

'I don't know.' He sounded startled. 'Camden doesn't like me, you see,' he added after a pause.

'And you think your talk with him may influence him to take some action against Henrietta? He won't, you know, unless he has more to go on than we know about.'

'You may be right.'

'I *am* right. And you must remember that when you saw him, you hadn't even seen Henrietta, let alone made up your mind about her.'

'I'd forgotten that,' said Antony meekly. 'Anyway, if necessary will you see her?'

'Yes, of course I will.' She looked at her husband and then back at Maitland again. 'Dominic and I asked you to take us on trust about Oliver,' she said, 'so I don't see why you shouldn't reciprocate in the case of this girl.'

'That's generous of you.'

'So . . . what next?'

'Three babies have died, and if we go on the theory of Oliver's innocence I think we have to assume that each murder was connected. Having cleared Henrietta Vaughan in my own mind we need a substitute, and that means finding out whether there's any other mentally disturbed person locally who might be guilty. I may say I asked Dera about this, if any other new mothers had lost their babies and been unduly upset about it, but she couldn't help me.'

'I don't think you can say "unduly upset", it would be an awful thing to happen,' said Lisa.

'Yes, I'm sorry, I meant someone who showed signs of being mentally disturbed by the fact. But you see it needn't be someone to whom that had happened, any psychiatric case . . . I wondered if your friend Martin Weatherby could help us about that. Someone recently released from a mental home for instance.'

'I don't think that's the kind of thing they put in the Chedcombe Herald, though I suppose he might have heard of such a person. I think the NSPCC would be a better bet. Someone whose children were in care because they'd been ill-treated. Something like that.'

'Of course you're right. That's just the sort of thing Vera would have come up with, she's one of the most logical people I know. Can I leave that to you, Lisa?'

'Yes, of course. I'll ask Martin too, just in case. Is there anything else?'

'Only if it's possible to find out whether there's anyone with a grudge against either of the Swifts or the Blunts. We're trying to do that in the case of Sandra Linwood's baby.'

'Yes, but that was to protect Oliver. If all the cases are connected . . . are you suggesting that two of them might have been a sort of coverup for a genuine motive, something to make people believe there was a madman or more likely a madwoman at work?'

'It's a possibility.'

'Nobody would be so – so cold-blooded.'

Antony smiled at her again. 'If you're going to take over the criminal side of your firm's practice, even in a place like Chedcombe you'll find there are lots of people who can be quite as cold-blooded as that,' he told her. 'And now let's talk of other things, because otherwise we'll be going over and over this business with no real knowledge to base our discussion on. What have you been up to today, Dominic?'

The rest of the evening passed quietly, the only surprise being Dominic's when he found that their visitor was well-informed and interested in farming matters. Antony was granted the privacy of a small room, obviously used as an estate office, to make his telephone call home. He found Jenny, as he had expected, dining with Sir Nicholas and Vera, but he cut their talk short and was non-committal when she told him that his uncle was demanding a progress report. He had a feeling there might be fireworks when he made it and tomorrow would be quite soon enough for that.

Sunday, 20th July

I

Maitland and Lisa walked down to the Saracen's Head at about eleven-thirty the following morning, and Ruth Jenkins the landlord's wife let them in by the side door. 'Of course Tom and I will be only too glad to help,' she assured them, leading the way to a snug sitting-room at the back of the house, 'but I can't for the life of me think how we can.'

Ruth and Tom Jenkins were one of those couples who had grown alike over the years, so that they might as easily have been taken for brother and sister as man and wife. Both had short curly grey hair and round amiable faces, though Tom, Lisa had assured Antony, was quite capable of keeping order on the rare occasions when that became necessary. 'It's a matter of trying everything,' said Antony, subsiding into a chair and accepting with gratitude a glass of bitter. 'I listened to the talk on Friday night, and local opinion seems strongly in Mr Linwood's favour. Would you agree with that?'

Ruth and Tom consulted one another with a look. This did not, he soon realised, indicate any doubt as to their reply, only as to who should respond to his question. Finally it was Tom who spoke. 'A hundred percent and then some,' he said. 'Not that Oliver doesn't have his odd little ways, not a bit like anyone else. He must seem strange to a chap like you from London, but we're used to him, you see.'

'I'm not altogether without experience of people's oddities,' Maitland murmured.

'No, of course not.' But Tom was intent on his narrative, and probably hadn't taken in what was said. 'The fact of the matter is he wouldn't hurt a fly' (it was only a matter of time before somebody besides Lisa had said this, Antony had felt sure) 'and

109

to tell you the truth he was quite proud of that new cousin of his, wasn't he, Ruth?'

'He was that. And he'd said often enough he hoped Sandra would have a boy, to let him off the hook as he put it. There'd be a Linwood still at the big house and nothing for him to worry about.'

'You knew about the entail then?'

'Yes, but I don't think anyone else in the village did. Certainly we never talked about it.'

'After the boy was killed?'

'He came down to tell us, and as a matter of fact he was here when the police arrested him.' Again it was Ruth who replied. 'But it had never occurred to him – I'd swear to this on the Bible, Mr Maitland – that anyone would think he'd done it. I don't think he'd even given a thought at that time of the change it would make in his circumstances, and it was too soon, was all too much of a shock for us to have started teasing him about the responsibilities he'd be undertaking.'

'Did he never think of marrying himself?'

'Always said it would be too much bother,' Tom put in. 'I suppose, Mr Maitland, we knew him as well as anybody did besides Dominic and Lisa here, along with his taking his meals with us sometimes. There'd be girls now and then we'd tease him about, and heaven knows what he got up to when he went into Chedcombe. I wouldn't have you thinking he was queer in that way.'

'The truth is he couldn't afford to get married,' said Ruth. 'And whether what he said was in the way of face-saving I couldn't tell you. But there it is, if he gets out of this mess things will be different, and whether he'll like it or not I don't know, but I think not.'

'Did you ever overhear anything in the bar that led you to think any local person had a grudge against either Mr or Mrs Walter Linwood?'

'Nothing like that at all. They didn't mix much locally, I think it was only your friend Mr Weatherby, Lisa, who was on visiting terms with them,' said Ruth. 'Oliver certainly never said a word against them, and even if there had been somebody with a grudge . . . who'd take it out on a child?'

110

'Somebody did.'

'That was that poor girl from Chedcombe, I daresay,' said Ruth. 'You have to be sorry for her, off her head with grief I wouldn't wonder. But no one in their right mind . . . you can take it from me, Mr Maitland, that's how it was.'

'So that story has got over here too, has it?' said Antony, apparently forgetting that the subject had been gone into pretty thoroughly on Friday night.

'You don't sound as if you believe me.'

'I do and I don't,' said Antony enigmatically, and though they talked for a little longer nothing at all was said that could, by any stretch of the imagination, be construed as being of the slightest use.

II

Lisa had made an appointment with Dr Clifford Elliott for two o'clock, so they set out for his house almost as soon as luncheon was over. On the way she told Maitland what little she knew of the man they were going to see, which was more or less what he had already heard from Martin Weatherby. Elliott was a widower of some years' standing and after the death of his wife had given up general practice to become administrator at St Luke's Hospital. 'I've always heard him well spoken of,' she said, 'and I believe Dad knows him, though exactly how intimate he was with the Linwoods I haven't the faintest idea.'

'You're telling me this might be another wild goose chase.'

'Yes I'm afraid it may, unless Martin was right and he was really close to them.' Lisa was quiet this afternoon, he had a feeling that perhaps she had been counting too much on what Ruth and Tom Jenkins might tell them.

'Never mind. At least seeing him won't leave us any worse off,' Maitland comforted her.

Their way took them a short distance back towards Chedcombe, across the main Chedcombe to Northdean Road, past another village and then through the gates of what seemed to be a large house. The drive was a long one, through grounds

111

beautifully kept, and the house, when they turned the final bend and it came into view, was a perfect example of Georgian architecture. Antony thought idly, there's money here, and the impression was confirmed when they were let into the house by – of all things! – a uniformed housemaid (another example of the heredity system Lisa had spoken of, perhaps) and led directly to a large and beautifully proportioned drawing-room. Maitland had no pretentions to being a connoisseur, but he would have been very much surprised to learn that anything in the room, whether furniture or ornament or painting, was anything but genuine and the best of its kind, while as for the carpet . . .

Dr Elliott had risen when they went in, marked his place carefully in the book he was reading, and laid it down on the table beside him. He was one of those men whose age is impossible to guess, and who would probably change not the slightest between the age of twenty-five and sixty. A tallish man, rather heavily built, with a beak of a nose but features that otherwise were almost classical. He was dressed casually, and Maitland's quick eye noticed that beside the book a pair of gardening gloves were apparently waiting for him. Perhaps that was his hobby, but he hadn't felt free to indulge it until after their visit.

'My dear Mrs Traherne,' said Dr Elliott coming towards them, 'this is a pleasure I've long awaited. I can't claim a close acquaintance with your father, but of course I do know him and he has spoken of you often.'

'It's a pleasure for me too,' said Lisa, not to be outdone in politeness, 'though I'm afraid we may be troubling you unnecessarily. This is Mr Maitland, who has accepted a brief to defend Oliver Linwood.'

Keen grey eyes turned in Antony's direction. 'So you're the famous "lawyer from London",' Dr Elliott said with a smile. 'You'll forgive me for using the local description, it has always amused me ever since I first heard of you when you defended the Gifford girl. I'm very glad to meet you at last, but I'm afraid you won't have so easy a time on this occasion.'

If Antony thought the description of the Gifford case as easy was rather a poor one he made no sign. 'Like Mrs Traherne,' he said, 'I hope we are not interrupting your leisure unnecessarily. As you seem to be aware, we shall need all the help we can get.'

'Then we'd better sit down.' He waited until they had accepted his invitation before sinking back into his own chair again. 'I think I should begin by telling you that I am completely in disagreement with the police over this matter, but I'm afraid my mere opinion goes for nothing and won't be of much assistance to you.'

'It's interesting to me though, coming into the affair as a stranger.' Lisa, after she had made the introductions, had made no attempt to take over the interview, but after all that was what she had wanted him for, wasn't it, to do the dirty work? 'Obviously you know Oliver Linwood then.'

'Mainly by reputation, though I have met him a few times, of course. It never occurred to me after what had been happening in Chedcombe that there would be any doubt as to who the guilty party was. Not that I'm blaming the girl, obviously she was not in her right mind when she did these dreadful things.'

'You're talking of Henrietta Vaughan, I suppose.'

'Who else?'

'May I ask you if you know her personally, Doctor, or if you are going by general repute?'

'I know of her only as a patient at St Luke's who lost her own baby and whose mind, I fear, gave way under the strain. She was an unmarried mother, with no one to turn to in her grief. Perhaps we should have realised what was happening, but I don't think we can be blamed for not considering anything so bizarre.'

'I took the liberty of speaking to Sister Mohamad at the maternity ward at your hospital yesterday, Doctor. She was definitely of the opinion that Miss Vaughan was not more than normally disturbed about what had happened. Certainly not to the point of madness. After all, it can't be easy for any woman to lose her child but particularly – as you pointed out – for an unmarried girl.'

'Sister Mohamad is an excellent nurse, but so far as I know she has had no psychiatric training.'

Maitland acknowledged the point with a slight inclination of his head. 'When did you first hear the rumours about Henrietta Vaughan, doctor?'

'I heard of her through normal channels when the baby was born dead. You will understand that such matters are no longer

113

any direct concern of mine, but I make it a practice to know what is going on in the hospital, and this was an unusual enough event for me to hear of it almost immediately. You will know perhaps that infant mortality is no longer quite so serious a problem as it once was.'

'So I understand,' said Maitland rather vaguely. 'But the rumours, doctor. When did they first come to your attention?'

'Quite soon after the second death. A Mrs Parker came to see me, a neighbour of the girl we're talking about. She said she was worried about Miss Vaughan, whom she described as a friend of hers, and wanted to know what she should do about it.'

'Excuse me, doctor, by worried do you mean worried that she might have committed these murders?'

'That's exactly what I do mean. She wanted my advice, so of course I told her the only thing she could do was to mention her fears to the police. If there was nothing in them, they would soon find out, whereas if she was right the girl must obviously be stopped.'

'Did she say in what way Miss Vaughan was behaving oddly?'

'Mooning about I think was the phrase she used. And talking wildly of the unfairness of everything, and generally not behaving in a rational way.'

'Then it is your opinion that all three murders were committed by the same person?'

'It is very definitely my opinion. By Henrietta Vaughan in fact.'

'The police don't agree with you.'

'So I gathered when I heard of Oliver's arrest. But what I have told you is unfortunately only an opinion, and I'm afraid it would have no value in law.'

'None whatever,' Maitland agreed. 'But in view of the police attitude I have no choice but to try to find some other rational motive for the Linwood child's murder other than my client's.'

'Yes, I can see that. If any motive for murder can be called rational. How can I help you?'

'I have heard your name mentioned as one of the few people who were intimate with the Walter Linwoods.'

'They are, they were I should say in Walter's case, a very fine couple and dear friends of mine. But how anyone who wasn't

114

deranged could have wanted to harm their child, particularly in the very sad circumstances ... that's something I simply can't believe.'

'All the same, doctor, I should be very grateful if you'd humour me. First of all perhaps, you would tell me something about these friends of yours.'

'I suppose I should begin by saying that I knew Walter's father too, and his uncle, Dr Andrew Linwood, though they were both a good deal older than I, just as I was a little older than Walter and Sandra. Walter took over the estate at quite an early age following the tragic accident that killed his parents. In fact I think he was only twenty-one at the time, but a very serious young man, and obviously cut out for the role he had to undertake. I don't remember exactly when he married, not until about two years ago I think, and that was when I first met Sandra. I have read enough detective stories to realise that you won't have been able to see her, though Mrs Traherne must have described her to you. A very beautiful woman, and Walter was very much in love with her, as she was with him. A perfect match, you might say.'

'You saw them quite often, I believe?'

'Certainly I did.'

'I was wondering, you see, whether Walter's death came as a complete surprise to you as it seems to have done to everyone else, except, I imagine, his own doctor.'

For a moment Dr Elliott stared at him. 'I don't quite know what that can have to do with the case,' he said with the first trace of coldness he had shown. 'It was obvious from his uncle's early death – Dr Andrew Linwood that is, your client's father – that there was some weakness in the family, and Walter spoke to me once or twice of things his own physician had told him. But childhood weaknesses are so often outgrown, the first news of his death came as a complete surprise to me. And, of course, a great grief. It was only later that I was able to think the matter through in a more reasonable manner.'

'His death was very sudden, I understand.'

'Very sudden. As a matter of fact ... but I don't know what this can have to do with the child's death, Mr Maitland.'

'Only that Oliver Linwood would have had no motive for

killing Walter's son, if Walter had not himself died first.'

'You're thinking that the prosecution will maintain that the matter was carefully thought out, from the time of Walter's death at least?'

'I'm quite sure they will, though no final plan could have been made until Mrs Linwood's baby turned out to be a boy.'

'But there's no chance, is there, of disproving that particular claim?'

'I'm afraid not, but it's the reason for my interest, and must be my excuse if my questioning seems to take an unexpected turn.'

'Then I'll tell you what I was going to say just now. I dined with Walter and Sandra myself the evening before he died and there was certainly nothing apparently wrong with him then. His own doctor, Robert Garfield, was there as well, as a guest, not in a professional capacity, and two other friends, Charles and Jean Colborne. It was a very pleasant evening, with Walter in particularly good spirits, and yet next morning Sandra phoned me in great distress to tell me that he was dead.'

'At such a time, with the birth of her baby so near, his death must have been particularly shocking to her.'

'Yes. I went straight out to Linwood House, of course, and had a word with Robert Garfield after I'd seen Sandra. I felt, as her time was so near, it would be better for her to come immediately into the hospital, but though he agreed with me about the possibility of a miscarriage he insisted that even so short a journey by ambulance might have a bad effect. So a nurse was arranged for her, and little Mark quite safely delivered at home. And then just when everything seemed to be going well—' He broke off shaking his head sadly.

'As you were such close friends it may be of some comfort to you to know that Oliver Linwood never had any intention of depriving Mrs Linwood of her home.'

Elliott looked up sharply. 'If he's found Not Guilty, as I sincerely hope he will be, she'll have no choice but to leave Linwood House,' he said.

'Whatever the verdict the position will be complicated,' Maitland told him. 'My acquaintance with the law of Entailed Interests is superficial, but I imagine if Oliver was free it would be open to him to make whatever arrangement he felt was

116

equitable for his cousin's widow.'

'Sandra has friends, she doesn't need his help.'

'Don't you think she might prefer it to being completely penniless and homeless?'

Dr Elliott looked a little taken aback. 'I had no idea—' he said, but went on without explaining himself further. 'If on the other hand Oliver is convicted, what would happen then?'

'The position would be one for the court to decide. I imagine that the estate would be dealt with as though the baby, Mark Linwood, had died intestate . . . which may sound silly, as what else could he have done at that age? But I don't see any other way of settling the matter.'

'And what would the result of that be?'

'Two sets of death duties, I imagine, but then his mother would inherit.'

'And the entail?'

'Would be lost, I imagine, in the confusion. Mrs Sandra Linwood would own the property free and clear, with no strings attached.'

'Then as her friend . . . this is very difficult,' said Dr Elliott, and divided a smile between his two visitors.

'You mean knowing where your sympathies should lie,' Antony suggested. And went on, when Elliott did not immediately reply, 'You were speaking of the Linwoods's friends other than yourself.'

'Yes, and what I meant when I said that Sandra wouldn't be left to face things quite alone was that, though they had few intimate friends among their wide circle of acquaintances, those they had were very close to them.'

'Besides,' said Maitland, carefully not catching Lisa's eye, 'Mrs Sandra Linwood is a young woman, and extremely attractive I've been told. There's every chance she'll marry again.'

'It's early days to be talking about that yet,' said Dr Elliott rather stiffly, 'with her husband dead a mere six weeks or so.'

'Yes, of course. I'm sorry if that sounded heartless, I was merely following your own concern for her well-being to its logical conclusion. Who would you say were their close friends besides yourself?'

'Robert Garfield and his wife to start with. He's their friend – I can't remember to say was in Walter's case – as well as their doctor. The Garfields live in Madingley, so I suppose you know them, Mrs Traherne.'

'Yes, quite well,' said Lisa, 'though fortunately we haven't had much business so far to put in Dr Garfield's way.'

'Was Mrs Garfield present at that dinner party, the night before Walter Linwood died?'

'No, the poor woman suffers from migraine, and that was one of the days it chose to strike her down.'

'You also mentioned a couple called Colborne.'

'Yes, Charles and Jean. He runs some sort of a business in Northdean, a successful one I gather, and they live on the outskirts . . . that is about twenty-five miles away from Madingley. I've also heard him speak of attending board meetings in London, so I imagine his interests are fairly wide. And from time to time, I've met Martin Weatherby at Linwood House, he's the editor of the *Chedcombe Herald*. A good enough sort of chap but with rather a taste for low company. I believe he's to be found in the Saracen's Head most evenings.'

Lisa opened her mouth to say something, but subsided again at a warning glance from Maitland. 'I've met Mr Weatherby,' he said non-committally. 'Also a couple called Blunt, who claim some acquaintanceship with Walter and Sandra Linwood.'

'I'm afraid I've never heard of them, though of course, it's possible I've met them at some time or other and not registered their names. But you've got me wondering, Mr Maitland, what is the precise purpose of this inquisition?'

'The strongest point the police have against Oliver Linwood is motive, and don't let anyone tell you that doesn't count even if it isn't supposed to legally. I think I said before, if there was anyone with a grudge against Walter, or more particularly against Sandra . . . it would need a twisted mind, but it might give me something to work on.'

'We've been talking about their friends.'

'To hate someone implies a certain intimate knowledge. But what I'm hoping, of course, is that someone who knew them may be able to suggest a reason for what was done.'

'Well, I don't think you'll get anywhere along those lines. I've sometimes thought Martin Weatherby had a – shall we say a soft spot for Sandra, so if it was Walter's death you were investigating . . . but that was quite straightforward. I'm only joking, of course, Weatherby's a solid citizen, completely trustworthy. But have you quite made up your mind, Mr Maitland, that Henrietta Vaughan didn't go over to Madingley that day?'

'I'm quite sure she didn't.'

'But that would bring us back to Oliver, wouldn't it? The man you're both trying to help.'

'He didn't do it,' said Lisa indignantly. 'You said yourself—'

'Yes, and I haven't changed my opinion. I have a great respect for Mr Maitland's judgement, as I'm sure you have, my dear, as you brought him into this business. But he doesn't know the background of the Linwoods' life as well as I do. If we separate the three murders, two on one side and one on the other, and absolve Henrietta Vaughan in the matter of Mark Linwood's death, I'm afraid we must come back to your friend and client, Oliver Linwood. I don't see any alternative, and my advice to you both would be to accept the obvious. It's the only way to help Oliver.'

'The obvious being that some lunatic encompassed all three deaths?' Antony enquired.

'Yes, and whatever your opinion of the Vaughan girl I'm afraid you will find that the theory of her guilt is psychologically sound.'

It was quite obvious that Lisa had prepared to argue with that, if it took all day. Maitland said pacifically, though not very originally, 'Well, we must agree to differ,' and, managed to get her out of the house before too much had been said. 'We mustn't alienate Dr Elliott any further,' he told her as they got into the car. 'I'm grateful to you for accepting my opinion of Henrietta, but after all the doctor is a partisan of Oliver's, and I'm afraid all we may have done is change his mind about that when he has time to think things over.'

'All you've done, you mean,' said Lisa rather coldly. 'And you weren't very tactful yourself, saying Sandra might marry again. After all, Dr Elliott had known Walter a lot longer than he'd known her.'

'Well, I'm sorry about that,' said Antony, not sounding in the least contrite. 'What about Martin Weatherby, do you think he might become one of her suitors?'

'No, I don't,' snapped Lisa. 'But even if a dozen people want to marry her why should they kill the baby? All that would accomplish would be to ensure that she'd be penniless and Oliver would inherit.'

'You're quite right of course, it doesn't make sense. Do you think it's worthwhile seeing the Colbornes, or will you drive me straight to the station at Northdean?'

'We'd be much too early for your train if we did that,' Lisa pointed out, and from her tone her spurt of temper was already evaporating. 'No, we'll do as we planned, but I'm beginning to feel pretty hopeless about it. If only you hadn't made up your mind so firmly about this girl Henrietta.'

'If and when you see her you'll understand what I mean,' Maitland assured her. 'All right then, on to Northdean and the Colbornes' house, and then you'll be able to rid yourself of me for a while. When do you think the case will come on, by the way?'

'Early in the Michaelmas Term,' said Lisa, slowing to make the turn into the main road to Northdean. 'I only wish,' she added, sighing, 'That the long vacation wasn't quite so long. It's going to be perfectly horrible for Oliver shut up all that time.'

'Yes, it's a pity,' said Antony, and forbore to point out that so far he could hold out no hope at all that things would be changed in that respect ever after the trial was over.

III

As they drove towards Northdean Lisa, probably intent on making amends for her strictures of a moment before, explained that Robert and Marion Garfield's house was on the opposite side of Church Lane to the row of cottages where Oliver had lived before his arrest. 'Of course Dr Garfield was the first person called when Sandra's baby was found dead,' she said, 'but it was a pathologist from Northdean who performed the autopsy. You'll find all the details of that with your brief.'

Maitland turned his head to smile at her. 'Yes, unfortunately,' he agreed. 'And we shall have to listen to all the unpleasant details at great length in court, whereas I am strongly of the opinion that any normal jury would be quite satisfied with the mere statement that the child was found asphyxiated, with his pillow over his face. However, far be it from me to suggest that we should ever ask them to take anything for granted.'

'Do you really expect anything to come from this visit to the Colbornes?'

If he'd answered that truthfully he'd have said, No, I'm just going through the motions. Instead he said, rather tritely, 'You never know what may be important until you try.' Which was also true, but probably conveyed more encouragement than he felt. And that was practically all that was said till they reached the outskirts of Northdean, where Charles and Jean Colborne lived on a brand new housing estate in what had every appearance of being extreme comfort.

The woman who let them in and identified herself as Jean Colborne was very small, with tiny hands and feet, but a body a little more rotund than it should have been. She had reddish hair and a face that was probably usually reasonably good-looking, though at present her expression was marred by something like a scowl. 'I can't think why Charles agreed to see you,' she said, as soon as Lisa had introduced the two of them. 'I was sorry about Sandra's baby, of course, particularly so soon after Walter's death,' – this was said so perfunctorily that Antony couldn't help thinking, she doesn't care a damn – 'but I thought all that was cut and dried. That dreadful cousin of Walter's—'

Maitland had realised long since that that was just the sort of remark calculated to make his instructing solicitor bristle, and probably come out with something decidedly tactless. He said, rather quickly and as ingratiatingly as he knew how, 'The law regards our client as being innocent until he has been proved guilty. I'm sure neither you nor your husband would want to hinder us from doing our best for him.'

She stood back then so that they could enter, and her manner showed some slight signs of thawing. 'I suppose to you it's just a job like any other,' she said. 'I can't say I'd like it, dealing with criminals all the time.'

'I'm sure you'll find, if you take the time to talk to Mrs Traherne, that most of her working hours are occupied with quite

121

innocuous things, such as conveyances and wills, and other such necessary evils.' He didn't glance at Lisa, but hoped fervently that she wouldn't take it into her head to contradict him. 'As for me, as you say it's a job, but it's also my duty to do it as well as I can.'

She surveyed him for a moment in a not altogether unfriendly way. 'Yes, Mr Maitland, I've heard of you,' she said, and suddenly she smiled. 'So has my husband. I hope it won't disappoint you too much to know that it wasn't in the interests of abstract justice that he agreed to talk to you, but purely out of curiosity.'

That, if either of his companions had known it, was the kind of remark to alienate Maitland irrevocably. However, with Lisa simmering gently at his side, he kept a firm rein on his temper and answered amicably enough, 'Be that as it may we won't take up much of your time. For one thing, I have a train to catch.'

Jean Colborne turned on her heel without a word and led the way into an elegantly furnished drawing-room. The chairs looked comfortable enough, but it was tidy, much too tidy, so that Antony would have given anything for the sight of one of the Sunday papers with its pages strewn haphazardly at the side of the chair of the man who rose to greet them. Charles Colborne was the complete antithesis of his wife, being tall and thin, and however he felt about the coming interview he managed a welcoming expression. He was, in fact, a rather good-looking man, but his dark hair was already receding a little, which probably made him look older than he was. Jean was attempting introductions, but he cut her short saying, 'Yes, my dear, I heard what you were saying in the hall. Do come and sit down, Mrs Traherne, and you too of course, Mr Maitland. I'm so very glad to make your acquaintance.' His eyes were on Lisa as he spoke, so that Antony thought, reprehensibly, a genuine, old-fashioned wolf.

Lisa took the hint and when Maitland maintained his silence, plunged into an explanation of their visit. 'You see,' she concluded, 'we're trying to find someone other than Oliver Linwood who might have had a motive for doing such a dreadful thing, and as we were told that you and Mrs Colborne knew the Walter Linwoods well we hoped you might be able to give us some hint about that.'

122

'You're going to be disappointed,' said Jean. She had been lingering in the doorway, but now came forward to join the group so that Maitland, who had been glad enough of an excuse to remain standing, had to follow her example and sit down. 'We've known Walter forever, but he was a solitary sort of chap, very wrapped up in the running of the estate. We both hoped – didn't we, Charles? – that when he married it would make a difference, but Sandra wasn't an easy person to make a friend of. They had masses of acquaintances, of course, she was a local girl though we hadn't met her until Walter introduced us, but I'd say we were the closest thing to intimates that they had.'

'I see you've taken our point, Mrs Colborne,' said Antony. 'For someone to harbour a grudge of such proportions, it must have been someone who knew them well.'

'Someone who knew Sandra very well I should have thought,' Jean corrected him. 'After all, Walter had been dead for a month when it happened.'

'In any case,' her husband put in, 'it doesn't seem to me to be necessary to look any further than Oliver, who according to Walter was odd enough for anything. And if you must look elsewhere surely the obvious place is Chedcombe. We've read about the murders there, it's obvious there's a lunatic of some sort at large.'

'Yes, and of course we're making inquiries on those lines. But we have to try everything, as Mrs Traherne explained to you.'

'But I'm afraid we can't help you. And I can assure you, Mr Maitland, if I were in any doubt of Oliver's guilt I should want to do my utmost. When I think of Sandra, losing husband and child within so short a time—'

'Sandra knows how to look after herself,' said Jean a little harshly, so that they all turned and looked at her. 'Well, I mean . . . of course I'm sorry for her,' she said, as though she realised for the first time how her previous remark had sounded. 'But I don't suppose for a moment that she'll grieve for Walter for ever, and as for little Mark, she'd hardly have had time to get used to having a child, particularly with all the people she had to help her look after him.'

'Jean dear, you're not thinking,' said Charles. 'They were a very happy couple and though I hope some day she'll find someone else—'

'She'll do that all right!' Jean almost spat at him.

'—have you thought what the position is at the moment? If Oliver is acquitted the whole estate will go out to him, except I suppose for whatever Walter was able to put aside out of his yearly income from it. That's right, isn't it?' he demanded of Maitland.

'Quite right.'

'But Oliver—' Lisa began, and again Antony interrupted her.

'If Oliver Linwood is convicted the situation will be extremely complicated.' He had no desire at all to impart information, but that was harmless enough and he said the first thing that came into his head to silence Lisa. 'Of course in the circumstances Mrs Traherne and I can't approach Sandra Linwood,' (he thought Jean mouthed the words, you haven't missed much, but couldn't be sure about that) 'but from what I've heard of Walter he sounds an excellent sort of fellow and I should have very much liked to have known him.'

'Not a town type at all,' said Charles.

'I was brought up in the country myself,' said Maitland, which was true enough though that part of his life had ended when he was thirteen years old, 'and my wife and I spend most of our summers on a friend's farm in Yorkshire.' Lisa gave him an inquiring look, but made no attempt to interrupt this flow of reminiscence, which she rightly guessed was not without its purpose.

'In that case, I imagine you'd have found yourself quite at home with him,' Charles agreed. 'It's a pity there's no one to show you round the estate. Though to tell you the truth,' he added confidentially, 'I think it was a little quiet for Sandra. She deserved something more, something a little more lively than the rather dull dinner parties they used to give. And go to, of course.'

'Such as the one you attended the night before Walter died, for instance,' Maitland suggested, making conversation, not really interested in the reply.

'Yes, that was dull enough,' said Jean. As she turned to look at her husband her tone became positively venomous. 'Though I didn't think you found it so. There was Sandra, looking as if the baby might arrive at any minute, and all you men hanging on every word she said, as if it was holy writ.'

124

'In the case of the two doctors, who I understand were the other guests,' said Maitland, 'I imagine if the event looked quite so imminent it was mainly professional interest.'

'Perhaps it was. But you're not a doctor,' she added accusingly, again addressing her husband.

'No, Jean, I'm not. I've often thought since that it was odd,' said Charles, obviously talking at random and trying to cover up his wife's only too obvious animosity, 'that on that particular night there should be two men with medical qualifications present, and neither of them with the faintest clue as to what was going to happen. Not that I ever think of Cliff Elliott as a doctor nowadays, since he gave up practising and went into administration at the hospital. But Walter was in particularly good form, all he could think of or talk about was the baby that was coming. I expect that's why my wife thought it was boring, she's happy enough usually with our social life.'

'I have to be, haven't I? All the same,' she went on, relenting, or perhaps feeling she had gone too far, 'I'm glad to think Walter was so happy that last evening. The estate meant a great deal to him, and he was hoping, of course, for an heir.'

'Yes, I can understand that must be a comfort now to his friends.' Maitland came to his feet as he spoke. 'I'm afraid you were right, Mrs Colborne, we've wasted your time for nothing. But it doesn't mean we're not grateful to you both for trying to help.'

It was Charles who went with them to the door. He seemed to be pondering something, and said when they were already on the doorstep, 'I don't know that you could exactly call it helping. You'll find that the police are right about Oliver, you see if I'm not right.'

'What a vixen,' said Lisa as she drove away. 'But she was quite right, you know, I can't see that it helped in the slightest.'

'It gave me perhaps a little more matter for reflection on the way back to town.'

She was slowing up as they reached the end of the drive. 'Do you remember which way we turned to get back to the main road?' she asked. 'I know once we get there we go left, and it's a straight run down to the station.'

'Turn left here too, and then take the first right,' said Maitland

125

positively. 'I didn't unroll a ball of twine as we came into this delightful suburb,' he added, seeing her suspicious look. 'I just happen to have a fairly good sense of direction.'

'Well, I hope that you're right, that's all,' said Lisa. But she followed his instructions obediently enough. 'What was in my mind, however, was what you said about having something to think about. What does that mean . . . is there anything I can tell Oliver?'

'If you mean anything hopeful, I wouldn't advise it. But I'm beginning to see certain – certain possibilities in the situation,' he admitted. 'You put those inquiries in hand that I asked of you, there's a good girl, and give me a call either in chambers or at home as soon as you've got something to tell me.'

'That's all very well—' Lisa started. But beyond what he had already said her companion refused to be drawn. He had a nasty fear that he had offended her in some way, but was a little reassured when she insisted on waiting with him for the train, and then kissed his cheek impulsively before he boarded it.

IV

The train was rather crowded, but no more than two minutes late. He got back to Kempenfeldt Square, therefore, in plenty of time for a drink before dinner, and wasn't surprised to hear that his uncle and aunt's customary Sunday teatime visit had been extended to cover the entire evening. In fact he'd have been extremely surprised to find anything else. Roger and Meg Farrell, who normally dined with them on Sunday, had gone down to their cottage at Grunning's Hole, so the four of them were alone together.

It was obvious from the first that not only Sir Nicholas, a notoriously impatient man, but also Vera, were anxious to hear what he had to tell them. Jenny too – and this surprised him – seemed disinclined to give him much leeway, and asked outright in the brief pause that followed their first greetings, 'Tell us what you've been doing, Antony. You're obviously looking into the matter, so I suppose your client must be innocent—'

'May be innocent,' Antony corrected her.

'—and the few scraps of information you've given me on the telephone only seemed to make Uncle Nick and Vera more confused.'

Maitland laughed aloud at that. 'In that case I suppose I've no choice but to put the record straight,' he said. 'And – you won't like this, Uncle Nick – there's just a chance I may have acquired another client in Chedcombe. At least, that Lisa may have and if she does I imagine that would mean a brief for me.'

Sir Nicholas eyed him suspiciously. 'I don't think I quite like the sound of that,' he said. 'Do you, my dear?' he asked his wife.

'Reserve judgement,' said Vera. 'Want to hear Antony's story in proper order. But tell me first, how is Lisa?'

'Very well and very happy I should say, except for this business of being quite convinced that Oliver Linwood is innocent. The baby's expected in January.'

'No complications there?'

'Not a one, I never saw a girl look better.' It was unlike Vera to require so much reassurance, but he ought to have known from Sir Nicholas's attitude that Lisa's well-being was very near his wife's heart.

'Dominic Traherne,' Vera went on with a question in her voice. 'Seems a nice young man, but I hardly know him.'

'He is, very nice. You don't need to worry about either of them, Vera, not personally that is. They're concerned about their friend, Oliver, and by an odd twist the entire village seems to be on his side too. None of that where there's smoke there's fire business, though I've met one or two other people who more or less took his guilt for granted. But I'd better tell you.'

'It would certainly seem to be desirable,' said Sir Nicholas, in the tone of voice which meant, and about time too. 'What little we've been able to glean from Jenny—'

'I never said I was any good at explanations, Uncle Nick,' Jenny protested. 'Only I did think . . . what is Oliver Linwood like, Antony?'

'I'd better come to that in correct chronological sequence,' said Antony, noting a rather ominous look in his uncle's eye. 'To begin at the beginning . . .' He had used his time in the train in part to put his narrative in order, for which he was now grateful.

Sir Nicholas, generally inclined to be captious on such occasions, listened almost in silence, although his nephew was uneasily aware that certain points were being taken note of without any particular pleasure, and would presently, no doubt, be used in evidence against him. 'So Lisa took me to catch the train in Northdean,' he concluded, 'and here I am.'

Sir Nicholas sat up a little straighter and deliberately picked up his glass, but none of them was in any doubt that he was about to bring his heavy artillery to bear. 'I take it from what you have told us that this girl, Henrietta Vaughan, is the other client of whom you spoke. May I point out to you, Antony, that her affairs are none of your business.'

'I went to see her because she might have proved a useful red herring,' said Maitland apologetically.

'If you must resort to colloquiallisms let it be to something a little more original,' said Sir Nicholas dampeningly. 'I take it too that though you still have some lingering doubts about the man who is your client, you have no doubt at all about *her* innocence of the crimes of which she may be accused. May I point out to you that such a conclusion can only be based on guesswork, and is, in any event, very unlike your usual state of indecision in such matters.'

Antony considered that for a moment. 'I've been thinking—' he began.

'Always a dangerous procedure,' said his uncle coldly.

'Well, you asked me what I've been doing, and that's one of the things. I *do* believe Henrietta, and I've finally come to the conclusion that I believe Oliver as well.'

'No doubt in due course you will give us your reasons for this change of heart,' said Sir Nicholas. 'However, at the moment I am more interested in the possible complications. Did either you or your instructing solicitor – who is a young girl, may I remind you, and should be able to look to you for guidance – consider the matter of conflict of interest?'

'Of course we did, Uncle Nick. Lisa knows as well as I do that our helping either of them depends on our being able to find out who really killed those babies.'

'You're treating the matter as one case then?'

'I think so, don't you? Madingley is only five miles from

Chedcombe, and though it's an agricultural district quite a lot of people who live there go to work in the town. And to think that there might be two murderers at work in such a small area, two murderers in the same line of business as it were –'

'I thought we had heard the last from you, Antony, of your dislike of coincidence.'

'No, Uncle Nick, I know they do happen, but this one's just too much for me to swallow. Not when you take all the other factors into consideration.'

'Such as the innocence of your – what was the unsuitable phrase you used? – your red herring,' said Sir Nicholas with distaste.

'Including that.' Antony sounded a little more cheerful, argument with his uncle was having its inevitable effect, but he got up restlessly, meaning to walk around the room a little. Catching his uncle's eye, however, he came to rest on the hearth-rug, his attention still concentrated on the older man. 'I've got Lisa looking into the possibility of a lunatic,' he said. 'Well, not necessarily a lunatic, somebody even temporarily deranged. I thought the NSPCC might be able to help, or the local psychiatric hospital.'

'Do you think you'll get a lead from that?'

It would normally have given Maitland great pleasure to annoy his uncle still further by alluding to the fact that that last question was less than perfectly worded. But he was uncomfortably aware of Vera's eyes fixed on him intently and concluded this wasn't the moment for playing the matador to Sir Nicholas's bull. 'No, I don't,' he said. 'I think the whole object of the exercise was the murder of the Linwood baby,' he added deliberately, 'and so long as Oliver's out of the running there'll be no more such deaths.' He turned a little to look directly down at Vera. 'I think Lisa told you,' he said, 'that she was worried in case the person responsible was at large when her own baby arrived. But I don't think she need worry about that, there'll be no more deaths.'

'You just told us you think Oliver's innocent.'

'Yes, Vera, but I'll be franker with you than I was with Lisa and Dominic. We haven't a hope of a Not Guilty verdict unless we can prove someone else's guilt. I'd rather get Oliver off

129

because, as I told you, I've come to believe him, but from a purely selfish point of view so far as the mothers in the region are concerned there's absolutely nothing more to worry about either way.'

'But you said—'

'I said I thought the whole point of the exercise was the Linwood baby's death,' Maitland repeated.

'That seems to get us back to Oliver again. Must say,' said Vera, who seemed to have rapidly recovered herself, 'he sounds a very queer fish to me.'

'Yes, he is, but a very likeable one.'

Sir Nicholas had been quietly watching his wife. Now he turned back to his nephew again. 'This latest statement of yours,' he said. 'I should like to know what brought you to that conclusion.'

'The dates when everything happened,' Antony told him. 'If you'd seen them written down as I have . . . here, I can show you,' he fished the original envelope he had used from his pocket, and it looked even more disreputable now. Sir Nicholas eyed it with some apprehension.

'I think on the whole, my dear boy, it would be better if you told us,' he said. 'To be asked to decipher your notes on top of everything else—'

Antony grinned. 'All right,' he agreed. 'Walter Linwood died of a heart attack on the morning of June ninth.'

'Which meant that from that time on the sex of his unborn child became of some importance.'

'Yes, but let's forget that for the moment.'

'In the circumstances, it would be rather difficult to forget it.'

'There can be more than one motive for murder, Uncle Nick. It doesn't have to be for gain.'

'Precisely,' Sir Nicholas agreed, with a decidedly unloving look.

'June the ninth,' Maitland repeated. 'Unexpectedly,' he added for good measure. He was amused to see that Vera had produced a notebook from her handbag and was solemnly writing down the dates as he gave them. 'The next thing that happened was that Henrietta Vaughan was delivered of a dead baby boy in the maternity ward of St Luke's Hospital, where, as I told you, Dera

Mohamad is now the Sister in charge. I've told you about my talks with both of them. Dera said the girl was upset but not more than she would have expected for someone of her type, quiet and rather nervous. Anyway it was just another tragedy, of no concern to anyone except the girl herself and her landlady, who seems to have more or less adopted her when her parents died. And to Dera, of course, who called to see her a couple of times to make sure all was well.'

'Does that mean she thought there might have been some mental upset?'

'No, Uncle Nick, I meant it when I told you that she was quite firm about the fact that Henrietta's reaction was perfectly normal. She was subdued in her manner, but what else would you expect? The next thing that happened was the kidnapping and murder of the Swifts' baby on the twentieth of June, followed rather quickly by the same thing happening to the Blunt baby on the twenty-third. Both cases were exactly similar except that one pram was wheeled away from the shopping centre, while the second was taken from the park while the mother was in the ladies' room. On the twenty-fifth of June, Sandra Linwood's baby was born at home, and he was killed on the eighth of July.'

Sir Nicholas reached out a hand, and his wife placed in it the paper on which she had been writing. He studied it for a moment. 'You have told us you believe all the deaths were connected,' he said, 'so I can only conclude that after Walter Linwood's death it became important to someone that his son, if he had one, should die too. To this end you are saying, I think, that the first two fatalities were intended to mislead the police into thinking some deranged person was responsible for everything that happened.'

'Yes, Uncle Nick, and it was just bad luck that Oliver chanced to be at Linwood House when Sandra's baby died.'

'You've still to explain who else could have had a motive.'

'We'll come to that in a moment.'

Sir Nicholas was still studying the list of dates. 'Is it also your theory that the intention was to blame Oliver for all these matters?' he asked.

'No, I don't think that at all. The rumour went round that Henrietta had been driven mad with grief over the loss of her child, and her desertion by his father, though if you ask me she'll get over that in time. There seems to be another boy friend waiting in the wings.'

That was an expression well known to infuriate Sir Nicholas. 'All this is very romantic, no doubt,' he said, 'but hardly to the point. You realise I'm sure that all you've told us so far only goes to strengthen the case against your client.'

'Yes, I do. And now you're going to say that the idea of killing his young cousin might have been put into his head by what had been happening quite independently in Chedcombe. The police believe that, or something very like it, and I'm only afraid—' He broke off there, but went on after a moment with defiance in his tone. 'I told you I'd seen Chief Inspector Camden. I certainly got the impression from what he said that he felt he had a strong case against Henrietta, and that an arrest wasn't far off. But what I don't like is the feeling that I may have made matters worse by suggesting to him that his theory was carrying coincidence a little too far.'

There was a moment's silence while Sir Nicholas studied his nephew. 'This talk with Camden, was it really necessary?'

'There were things I wanted to know that I hoped he could tell me.'

'You've come up against him before, I have the impression that he's a man who dislikes anything that he feels is interference.'

'Of course he does. And what's more he knows this chap Godalming who's AC (Crime) at the Yard now. If you remember he comes from those parts – Godalming, I mean – and was Chief Constable of Westhampton for a while before he got his present post.'

'What a knack you have for making friends,' said Sir Nicholas sarcastically.

'That's very unfair, Uncle Nick,' said Jenny. 'You know perfectly well—'

'Yes, my dear, but I was referring to the constabulary. What exactly did Inspector Camden have to say to you, Antony, besides the small amount of information you seem to have wrung out of him?'

Maitland met his look squarely. 'He warned me to stick to an orthodox treatment in my brief,' he said deliberately.

'It seems to be a little late for that now,' said Sir Nicholas dryly.

'But Uncle Nick, you said before ever I went down to Chedcombe—'

Sir Nicholas smiled and seemed to have undergone one of his abrupt changes of mood. 'I'm glad, of course, that you're taking your responsibilities to your client so seriously,' he said, 'but surely it could have been done without making yourself quite so unpopular?'

'I doubt it. No, really, Uncle Nick—'

'What is really troubling me,' said Sir Nicholas, and for once the gentleness of his tone did not seem to Antony to presage disaster, 'is your partisanship for this girl, Henrietta Vaughan. If you're wrong—'

'I'm not wrong, Uncle Nick, that's one thing I'm absolutely sure of.'

'Have you told Lisa that?' Vera put in.

'Yes, of course.'

'Have you also told her you feel she's no further cause to worry about there being someone abroad who's murdering babies?' Vera insisted.

'Well . . . no. I only really thought that out in the train coming home. I will tell her though, we'll be talking on the telephone before long.'

'I think that will be a very good idea,' Vera told him.

'Yes, so do I. Don't worry, Vera, I'll do my best to set her mind at rest.'

'Then perhaps it's time you told us your alternative suggestions to your client's guilt,' said Sir Nicholas. 'Jenny will give us another glass of sherry . . . we are not letting your dinner spoil, are we, my dear?'

'No, Uncle Nick, I turned the oven low and another half hour won't hurt anything.' She got up immediately to fetch the decanter. 'Besides, I want to know just as much as you do.'

'Then I'll do my best.' Maitland held out his glass, and then turned to put it on the mantel beside the clock. 'The trouble is,' he added in a worried tone, 'there are too many possibilities, and too many objections against all of them.'

'All the same,' said Sir Nicholas, 'I think we should all be obliged if you would be kind enough to give us the benefit of your ideas.'

'On the strict understanding that you won't at this stage accuse me of guesswork,' said Maitland. 'I shall really be doing no more than speak my thoughts aloud.'

'As on so many occasions,' said his uncle in a resigned tone, and gave an exaggerated sigh. 'However—' He gestured, as though graciously giving permission to proceed. Antony hesitated only a moment before responding.

'I suppose that from a common sense point of view the last woman we saw, the one Lisa prefers to call a vixen, should head the list.'

'I imagine you mean by that that she is the last person you yourself would suspect,' said Sir Nicholas ironically. 'Where common sense is concerned . . . but please go on, my dear boy, go on.'

'I'm talking about Jean Colborne. She and her husband seem to be among the few close friends the Walter Linwoods had, and Charles Colborne showed definite signs of admiring Sandra, though I've no means of knowing whether his wife's resentment of that fact was justified. However, resent it she certainly did, and I don't see how Sandra could have failed to realise the fact. But Walter had been their friend before he married, and as he sounds to have been an unimaginative sort of chap he may well never have given the matter a thought. Sandra . . . well, I shan't see her until we get into court, and I've no idea what makes her tick. She may have married Walter for love and stayed in love with him or she may have liked the comfortable financial background he could provide. Either way it would explain her wanting to please him by not quarrelling with Jean. Another possibility might be the one suggested by something Charles Colborne said, that Sandra found the kind of life Walter preferred to live a little dull and would welcome the company even of people she didn't particularly like.'

'The last part of the statement I presume is conjecture only.'

'Yes, sir, it is, but don't say I didn't warn you. Colborne did suggest that Sandra deserved a rather more lively existence than the one she led, but certainly made no suggestion that there was a falling out, or the possibility of falling out, between her and his wife.'

'I see. You're suggesting that Charles Colborne's real or imagined attentions to Sandra Linwood may have raised his wife's resentment to the point of paranoia, so that she might have murdered the baby by way of revenge.'

'I said it was a possibility, Uncle Nick. If revenge was the motive, and there was no intention of making Oliver the scapegoat, Sandra would have been deprived of child, home, and income at one stroke.'

'And the two previous murders were committed purely as camouflage, to suggest the existence of some unfortunate person the balance of whose mind was disturbed?'

'I do think that, sir, whoever was the murderer.'

'With reference to this theory about Mrs Charles Colborne, you spoke I believe of common sense. I shudder to think what the rest of your speculations may involve,' said Sir Nicholas, and refreshed himself with a sip of sherry.

'It gets worse as it goes on,' said Antony cheerfully. His uncle eyed him with disfavour.

'So I imagine,' he said. 'However, having invited your thoughts on the subject I suppose the least we can do is listen.'

'If you'd like me to stop—' Maitland offered.

'Don't be silly, Antony,' Jenny begged. 'You know Uncle Nick doesn't mean a word of it, and anyway what about Vera and me?'

'We then turn,' said Maitland, with a wary eye on his uncle, 'to the two other couples who lost their babies. Jenny love, I know you realise that apart from my talk with Henrietta Vaughan this was the most difficult part of the whole proceeding.'

'I still want to know what conclusions you reached about them,' Jenny told him. 'You see, I agree with Vera that it's important to set Lisa's mind at rest, and it seems you can do that if she trusts you.'

'She kissed me good-bye,' said Maitland smiling at her.

'That's a good sign,' said Jenny, returning his smile. 'But you've always said what a place Chedcombe was for gossip so I don't suppose there's a mother in the whole town who isn't terrified out of her wits for her own baby.'

'Yes, but they've settled on Henrietta as the murderer, so if my guess is right and Camden does proceed to an arrest their fears will be laid to rest. Just as we hope Lisa's will, though for another reason.'

'Yes, I see that. Even so, Antony, I want to hear.'

'John and Louise Swift are a young couple and were obviously very much wrapped up in their infant son. But they have courage,' (he was speaking directly to Jenny but did not add, though he would have liked to, as much courage as you have) 'and are looking to the future. The other couple, Ernest and Caroline Blunt, are quite a different kettle of fish. I learned later that they've got three children already, all old enough to be away at school, and Mrs Blunt confided in Dera Mohamad that the new baby was a mistake. I'd already gathered a what-is-one-among-so-many attitude, and that just went to confirm it.'

'But, Antony, their own child!' said Jenny, horrified.

Looking at her for a moment her husband's mind went back to the day he had visited her in hospital after her miscarriage, to her hand lying limply in his, and her voice saying weakly (not in reproach, though being the man he was a feeling of guilt had haunted him ever since) 'I thought you were dead.' He spoke to her as though they were alone together, 'Jenny, love, I wouldn't do anything deliberately to hurt you.'

'It's a long time ago,' said Jenny, just as though she had read his thoughts. 'Go on, Antony, I'm sorry I interrupted. But do you really think—?'

'I'm talking about possibilities,' he assured her, 'and I said there were objections to all of them. No, I don't think Carrie Blunt is likely, and if she had tried to raise a smoke screen she'd have stopped with the Swift baby, and not bothered to go over to Madingley as well. But they knew the Walter Linwoods, though not, I think, as well as they tried to imply, so even that remains a possibility.'

'We have now left the realms of common sense, Jenny,' Sir Nicholas assured her. 'If ever we were in them,' he added.

'I did warn you,' said Maitland. A last glance at his wife assured him that her serene look was back. She was sitting quietly beside Vera with her hands folded in her lap, and as he turned back to address his uncle again it occurred to him for the first time that Vera had been strangely quiet ever since he had been able to convince her that it should be possible to dissipate Lisa's fears. 'The Linwoods don't seem to have had many close friends,' he said, 'but there is a sort of hint in the village gossip that Sandra may not prove inconsolable for long. Certainly Jean

Colborne resented the attention she got, not only from Charles Colborne but from the rest of the men at that last dinner party, the night before Walter Linwood died. I pointed out that two of the men concerned were doctors, and might therefore have had a professional interest in Sandra's condition, seeing that her baby was due in a fortnight. But she wasn't having any of that.'

'Who were these men?' asked Sir Nicholas. He succeeded in sounding genuinely interested and Antony was suddenly aware of an enormous sense of gratitude that his family, Uncle Nick and Vera alike, were almost as concerned as he was himself for Jenny's peace of mind.

'Sandra's own doctor from the village, whose wife was laid up with a migraine. Charles Colborne, of course, and a Dr Clifford Elliott, who has given up the practice of medicine to become administrator at St Luke's Hospital in Chedcombe. Though he wasn't present that night I might also mention at this stage Martin Weatherby, who is the editor of the local paper, though he too lives in Madingley and is a fairly close friend of Lisa and Dominic's. Also, I think, from what Jean Colborne said, of the Walter Linwoods.'

'I don't quite follow you, I'm afraid,' said Sir Nicholas. 'You're implying that any one of these men may have been in love with Sandra Linwood . . . I'm aware that jealousy takes strange forms, but to kill her child seems to be carrying it to extremes. There's also the fact that even after Walter Linwood's sudden death in the case of the married men—'

'I told you I was just tossing around a few ideas,' said Antony. 'I don't know anything about Dr Garfield's wife, though I can well imagine Charles Colborne wanting to get rid of his. But we aren't just considering the baby's murder,' he added deliberately. 'I have to admit to a growing suspicion that Walter Linwood did not die a natural death.'

There was a moment's silence before Sir Nicholas said, 'My dear boy, have you faintest grounds for that suggestion?' This time the gentleness of his tone definitely boded no good.

'Nothing that I could prove. Nothing, I suspect, that would be susceptible of proof. It's happened before, a man with a known heart condition, a substance whose effects simulate those of a heart attack, the death certificate signed in perfectly good faith.'

137

'But he died suddenly, you say. In that case surely there would have been an inquest.'

'No, I don't think so, Lisa would have mentioned it, and the talk in the village pub would certainly not have ignored it. He was presumably under his doctor's care, and Dr Garfield obviously suspected nothing wrong.'

'Unless he was your hypothetical murderer,' Vera put in.

'If it was out of love for Sandra, Mrs Garfield would still be in the way,' Maitland pointed out.

'That would apply also to your other married suspect, in which case I suppose we must expect another "natural" death before long.' Sir Nicholas's tone was slightly sarcastic, but it was obvious that in spite of himself he was beginning to take an interest in the problem. 'You have mentioned four men who might have taken an interest in Mrs Linwood, three of whom were at dinner that night. If poison were administered . . . what exactly did you have in mind?'

'I haven't had time to refresh my memory, but I did have to look up digitoxin once, and in a man with a known heart condition the death might very well be put down as natural. But I haven't gone into this aspect of the matter at all, it's not impossible that the fourth man visited the house earlier in the day, and if Walter Linwood was taking some medication an opportunity might have occurred to add some noxious substance to it. I'm not wedded to the idea of digitoxin, but it has certain attractions.'

'Assuming for a moment that this particularly blatant piece of guesswork is correct,' said Sir Nicholas, 'surely one of the three men present at the house that evening is the most obvious choice. And as two of the men were doctors, with both the knowledge and the opportunity to obtain what was necessary—'

'It doesn't follow, Uncle Nick,' Antony interrupted. 'One of the few things I remember about the stuff is that a distillation can be made from the common foxglove. So we can't rule any of them out on that score.'

'I stand corrected.' Sir Nicholas definitely did not care for being interrupted. 'Let us take the matter a little further. We have four men, two bachelors—'

'Widowers, Uncle Nick,' said Maitland, compounding his error.

138

'Two men free to marry,' Sir Nicholas corrected himself, coldly, 'and two married men whose wives, as you pointed out, are not immortal. If one of these men wishes to marry Walter Linwood's widow, can you suggest any conceivable reason why he should wish her to be penniless when he does so?'

'Perhaps he doesn't like children,' Antony suggested. Argument with his uncle, besides raising his spirits, had occasionally the unfortunate effect of inducing in him a marked flippancy of manner. Sir Nicholas gave a snort of disgust, and his nephew added hastily, 'You're quite right, of course, it doesn't make sense, but I still have this very strong feeling—'

'May be right about the death being murder and wrong about the motive,' said Vera. 'If Sandra didn't marry him for love, or if she'd fallen out of love with him again, what's to say *she* didn't do it? Remember quite well about this foxglove business, there was nothing to stop her doing it any more than any of the others, and naturally – in case any suspicion arose – she'd choose an evening when they'd had guests.'

'Unfortunately there's an objection there too,' said Maitland. 'My impression of the lady is that she likes the good things of life and the village is definitely of the opinion that that's why she married Walter Linwood. So even if she could have brought herself to infanticide, why should she have beggared herself by killing her son?'

'Brings us back to Oliver,' said Vera. 'Know you don't like the idea of two murderers, but he might have been the one who tried to obscure the issue by killing the children in Chedcombe.'

'I don't like the idea of two murderers,' said Maitland stubbornly.

'Wouldn't really be a coincidence, one thing leading to another,' Vera insisted, shifting ground a little. 'But if you ask me,' she added, 'you'd better forget all about this idea of Walter Linwood, and concentrate on the murders you do know happened.'

'You're quite right, of course,' said Antony meekly. He turned to take his glass from the mantelshelf with his left hand and raised it in a silent toast that took in each one of his companions. 'If no one has any more questions, I'm hungry if you aren't,' he told them.

Sir Nicholas gave him a suspicious look. Jenny got up and

made for the door. Vera said in her gruff way, 'Think we've covered everything, but you needn't put yourself out to phone Lisa to set her mind at rest. Think I can explain your reasoning to her in a convincing way.'

V

It had been obvious to all of them ever since Antony came in that he was tired and that his shoulder, as so often happened on those occasions, was hurting him more than usual. Sir Nicholas and Vera therefore, by common consent, went home quite early. 'Do you really want to go to bed at this hour, Jenny?' Antony asked, coming back into the living-room after seeing them out.

'Not unless you do,' said Jenny obligingly.

'I just thought . . . you've been seeing a good deal of them, and perhaps you can explain. The situation seems to have changed since I went away, or rather Vera's attitude to it, and consequently Uncle Nick's.'

Jenny left her task of piling glasses on the tray, and sat down on the sofa again, patting the cushion beside her encouragingly. She did not, however, reply directly to his question. 'How do you mean?' she asked.

'They wanted me to go to Chedcombe because Lisa, and Dominic too, were worried about their friend Oliver Linwood,' said Maitland, speaking slowly and thinking it out as he went. 'It's perfectly true, they are, and with some cause. The bait held out – if I may put it that way – was that there was some danger of an innocent man being convicted of a crime he didn't do.'

'They know you very well, you see,' said Jenny.

'Yes love, but now it seems that Vera's real cause for concern was wanting to get the matter cleared up, one way or another, before Lisa had her own baby and had to start worrying about whether some madman might harm it. You saw the way she jumped at my explanation of why there was no further cause for worry on that score. I know she wouldn't want Oliver to suffer for a crime he didn't commit any more than I do, but it's the change in emphasis that I don't understand.'

Jenny was silent for so long that he began to think she wasn't going to answer. Presently her hand came out and found his, gripping it as though it formed a source of strength. 'I can explain that to you, Antony,' she said. 'Vera told me I might, in fact she said it was only fair to you that you should know about it, and this way it would be easier for her.'

'My dear and only love,' said Antony, bewildered, 'what in heaven's name are you talking about?'

'Well you see, Antony,' said Jenny, 'Lisa Traherne is Vera's daughter.'

'*What?*'

'Lisa Traherne is Vera's daughter,' Jenny repeated patiently.

'I heard what you said, but I can't quite take it in. Does Uncle Nick know?' he asked anxiously.

'Of course he does. You know Vera, she's the most honest person alive, she'd never have agreed to marry him without telling him that.'

'When he proposed to her you mean?'

'If you're thinking it would have been a bit late then for him to back out of it without looking like a cad,' said Jenny, putting her finger neatly on exactly what he was thinking, 'of course not. Any woman could have seen what was coming, I certainly could. She told him that morning they went to listen to the music at the Greek Orthodox Church.'

'Very appropriate.' Antony's tone was a little dry. 'But . . . Vera!'

'She was young once, you know,' said Jenny rather severely. 'But I admit she wasn't exactly a young girl when Lisa was born. There was no real reason for her to tell us now, but she said she felt she owed it to you when you were going out of your way to help.'

Maitland was beginning to get over his sense of shock. 'It explains one thing at least,' he said. 'I always had a feeling I'd met Lisa somewhere before. But does she know about it?'

'No, of course not. I'd better explain what happened,' said Jenny.

'I was afraid of that,' her husband told her, smiling.

'Of course if you don't want to hear . . . oh well,' she said, relenting. 'You remember Vera telling us she had a brother who

141

died at Dunkirk.'

'I remember you telling me that she'd told you,' said Antony precisely.

'That doesn't matter. This brother had a very close friend who wrote to Vera at the time but wasn't able to get to see her. There wasn't much leave going at the time, and then he was sent abroad again, and the war was over before he was able to get down to Chedcombe. I got the impression he'd promised his friend to give her a message in person, something like that, but anyway one thing led to another and they parted good friends and when she found she was pregnant Vera never told him. She said there'd never been any question of marriage between them, he was quite a bit younger than she was. So she went away quietly and had her baby – she never told me what story she'd made up to explain her absence to her friends – and put it up for adoption. And as luck would have it Lisa was adopted by a solicitor in Chedcombe called Williams and his wife, both of whom she knew well, which I suppose is one of the coincidences you're so set against. So she's always been able to watch Lisa's progress, and to become friends with her after a while. Does Lisa know the Williamses aren't her real parents?'

'Yes, but I don't think it's a thing she ever worries about. You may not know she's in partnership with her father now, I mean with Ralph Williams.'

'And she's never shown any curiosity—?'

'About her real mother? None at all as far as I can see, not that it would do her much good. But Vera's a wonderful woman, she'd never do anything to interfere with the happy relationship that exists between Lisa and her adoptive parents. Only I can understand her being concerned about her coming grandchild.'

'You were able to set her mind at rest about that, nobody's going to murder it,' said Jenny. 'And you needn't even ring up to explain your reasoning on the point to Lisa, because Vera's decided to do it for you.'

'Yes, I know, but . . . do you know, love, I think I may have to go back to Chedcombe again? If I can find time before the vacation, that is.'

'You've got an idea,' said Jenny, almost as though it were an accusation.

'The glimmerings of one. You understand, Jenny love, if I try to expound it to you it'll probably go away. And if you must blame anyone,' he added, smiling at her, 'blame Uncle Nick. Arguing with him is always stimulating. And I shall only go if what I'm afraid of happens and Henrietta is arrested,' he added in a cajoling tone.

'I understand you're worried about her, but why would that make a difference?'

'Because it isn't going to break Oliver Linwood to spend the two or three months before the trial can come on in prison.'

'But you like him,' said Jenny before he could go any further.

'Yes, I do, love, and so would you if you met him. But I have to admit he's not at all like anybody else, and though I don't suppose he's enjoying himself at all he's the sort of person who can make himself content with very little, and the fact that he can't get out isn't a major consideration to him. But Henrietta's different, it would be a sheer tragedy to her.'

'Then of course you must go.'

'I admit I'd rather deal with the matter in court,' he said, as though she hadn't spoken, 'and even if I do try to force matters it may come to that.'

'Antony, what do you mean to do?'

'Nothing you need worry your head about. A few questions asked in the right places to confirm what I'm beginning to suspect.' He smiled again and pulled her a little closer to his side. 'If I convince myself,' he told her, 'I can probably persuade Camden too.'

'He sounds an awfully obstinate man,' said Jenny doubtfully.

'As to that, I can be obstinate myself. Jenny love, you needn't worry, I promise you I won't do anything stupid.'

'Of course not,' replied Jenny dutifully, and didn't remind him of all the occasions when he had told her practically the same thing, just as sincerely as he was doing now, and been proved wrong.

Wednesday, 23rd July

Maitland got back from court the following Wednesday afternoon to find a message that Mrs Traherne had phoned, but when he tried to return the call her clerk informed him that she had already left for home, but it would probably be as well not to call her immediately as she meant to do some shopping on the way. He had already worked exhaustively on the brief that would take him back to court tomorrow, so this seemed a good enough excuse to take an early night himself. If Lisa had something to communicate she would be sure to ring again; if she didn't he would get in touch with her himself.

He and Jenny would be alone that evening, as Meg and Roger were still at Grunning's Hole. Meg, better known to her admirers among the theatre-going public as Margaret Hamilton, was resting longer than usual this time, to her husband's great delight, and though she did her best to share Roger's enthusiasm for sailing all her acting ability couldn't quite hide the fact from Antony, who had known her for a very long time, that she preferred their excursions to take place when the weather was fair. The recent spell of sunny days with very little wind had no doubt encouraged her to persuade him to stay away from his business at the stock exchange for longer than he had intended. They might be in the cottage, and they might have taken to sea in the *Windsong* for a longer period. Either way it was high time Roger had a break by having his wife's undivided attention for a longer spell than usual.

The previous evening as custom dictated, Sir Nicholas and Vera had dined with them. After Jenny's revelations Antony had a faint fear that some awkwardness might have arisen between himself and Vera, but was relieved to find that everything was just as usual: Sir Nicholas demanding to know if he had had any

144

further thoughts on the Linwood case, and being his caustic self on hearing of his nephew's intention to make another trip down to Chedcombe before the long vacation if his fears had been realised and Henrietta Vaughan had been arrested. Obviously his report that Lisa's personal fears could now been laid to rest had something to do with that. Vera's worry had been for her daughter's peace of mind, Sir Nicholas's for his wife's. Things could now return to normal and the normal thing would have been to let the matter run its course and wait for the trial, or possibly trials, in the Michaelmas term. 'If you could reasonably expect to achieve anything at this stage I might possibly agree with you,' said Sir Nicholas inaccurately. 'But I suppose reason is the last thing I should expect after knowing you so long.'

Maitland agreed with him meekly enough, being a prey to considerable doubts himself, and the matter was allowed to drop.

Lisa's shopping couldn't have taken very long, because he hadn't been home ten minutes before the phone rang and he heard her voice at the other end of the line. She sounded excited, or if that was too strong a word not quite her usual calm self. 'It's just as you thought,' she told him almost before he had time to return her greeting. 'That girl, Henrietta, has been arrested.'

'When?'

'This morning. Your friend Minnie phoned me, she's a sensible person, and I went round and stopped Henrietta saying anything to the police. So what do you want me to do now?'

Maitland had had plenty of time to think this out. 'You can handle the Magistrates' Court hearing,' he said. 'Don't ask any questions, don't introduce any witnesses of course, just plead Not Guilty and reserve your defence. At least' – a sudden doubt assailed him – 'those are your instructions, aren't they, that she didn't do it?'

'And I thought you were so sure!' Just for the moment there was a tinge of amusement in her voice.

'I was . . . I am.'

'Well, I'm glad of that, because having seen Henrietta I agree with you. Anyone in her situation would feel dreadful but there's nothing abnormal about her, given the sort of person she is. You were wrong about one thing though, she almost welcomed being arrested.'

'But she's such . . . such a timid little thing I should have said.'

145

'She's not particularly little, though she's certainly timid. That's the whole trouble. She's been living cooped up because she couldn't bring herself to show her face outside the house, and just rushed upstairs and shut herself in her room every time anyone called. I went back afterwards and talked to Minnie, and she says that boy you mentioned, Eddie, still wants to marry her, and she's sure Henrietta would agree if everything were cleared up. As it was she wouldn't even see him.'

'So much for my attempt to talk some sense into her,' said Antony sadly. 'Anyway, Lisa, we've got as far as the Magistrates' Court.'

'Yes, I can handle that, but what next? Will you take the brief?'

'Probably, in the long run. I've been thinking over that conflict of interest business, and I don't see that it would necessarily arise. If Oliver Linwood is tried first, which seems the most likely thing, and if we've nothing more to go on than we have now, we can still raise the two cases in Chedcombe by way of red herrings, and as Henrietta's case will still be *sub judice* no one will be able to bring her name into it. In fact, if the jurors have got it firmly fixed in their minds – their collective mind I should say – that she's guilty maybe it'll be all to the good. I think we'll have to ask for a change of venue in her case, but that can wait. Anyway as far as her defence goes, whether Oliver is found innocent or guilty, we shan't be any the worse off.'

'No, I see that,' said Lisa rather slowly. 'But why won't you accept the brief now?'

'Because I'm coming down to Chedcombe again, tomorrow evening if the case I'm engaged in finishes in time, and I want a free hand to ask questions of people whom, as Henrietta's lawyer, you won't be able to see.'

'You mean the woman who started all the trouble, Marilyn Parker?'

'Yes, exactly.'

'I did think of going to see her, before Henrietta was arrested I mean. But then I couldn't see what good it would do.'

'That's what I thought when I was in Chedcombe before, but now . . . it's just that I have a sort of idea,' said Maitland rather apologetically. 'Nothing positive enough to put into words,' he added quickly, 'but there's just a chance that she may be able to help me.'

146

'Well, I did do the other things you asked, talking to the doctors in the psychiatric ward of the hospital, and even going out to the County Psychiatric home. Nobody at all seems to have been released from either place recently, let alone anyone with tendencies that might have led them to – to do what was done.'

'Nobody at all? That sounds rather unusual.'

'One of the doctors quoted to me a case from somewhere up north that happened a few months ago. A woman who'd murdered her son, a young man I think, not a baby, and after a few years they thought she was cured and released her and she went straight home and killed her husband. So everybody's been taking particular care since then.'

'I'm not surprised. What about the NSPCC?'

'They couldn't help either. They had the usual quota of cases of child abuse of course, and some where children have been taken into care and placed in foster homes, but all the parents concerned seemed to have left the district, except for one woman who the caseworker was quite sure had nothing to do with what happened. Her husband had been the trouble, generally when he was drunk, and he'd left her and disappeared at least six months ago.'

'I see. Well, there's always the chance that on that front at least something else may come up before the trial comes on, something the social workers know nothing about at the moment. In any case, it won't do any harm to harp on the possibility a little.'

'I did one other thing,' said Lisa rather tentatively. 'I had a word with Dr Garfield.'

'Did you indeed? Good girl!'

'It was Vera's suggestion actually when she rang me up on Monday. And he's our doctor, of course, though until I became pregnant we'd neither of us ever needed his services. So when I went to see him for a checkup I very casually brought the subject round to what a dreadful thing it was that Walter Linwood had died so soon before his son was born.'

'Was he willing to talk about it? Not from a medical point of view, I realise that, but as a guest who was at the house that evening.'

'Yes, but what he had to say wasn't anything to get excited about. He only confirmed what you'd heard before from Dr Elliott and that ghastly Colborne woman. Walter was full of

147

pleased excitement, hoping the child would be a boy, of course, because of his pre-occupation with the estate and the family name, but either way he'd be happy, there was plenty of time to remedy matters if Sandra had a girl. Poor man, it's a good thing he couldn't see into the future. I gathered, but of course Dr Garfield didn't say so, that he wondered whether it might have been getting so worked up that put the final strain on Walter's heart. But I still don't understand why you wanted to know about that evening.'

'I think we'll save it until I see you,' Antony told her. 'If I can get away tomorrow I'll call you from the station, or have my clerk let you know if I haven't got time for that.'

'You'll stay with us, of course.'

'No Lisa, though I'd like to. I think in the circumstances it might be open to misinterpretation, a sort of admission on my part that I intended to accept the brief to defend Henrietta. So don't think of meeting me, I'll stay at the hotel as I've done before and come round to your office around nine-thirty, say, the following morning. All this is assuming the jury don't take too long to make up their minds tomorrow, but it's an open and shut case really, I don't think they'd have much difficulty in finding my unfortunate client Guilty.'

'All right then, I'll see you on Friday with luck. There's just one thing I did get out of my talk with Dr Garfield,' said Lisa a little hesitantly.

'What was that?'

'He didn't say it in so many words because of course we couldn't discuss the case against Oliver, as he was the first person called when the baby was found dead and will be giving evidence for the prosecution. But I'm pretty sure he doesn't think Oliver's guilty. It isn't so surprising really, after all he's known him all his life and was on good terms with his mother – so Dominic tells me – as being the widow of one of his predecessors. I just thought that you might like to know that he's not likely to be making any unpleasant remarks on the side, that the judge would order stricken from the record, but of course the jury would have already made a mental note of them.'

'No, that is comforting.'

'I wish you'd tell me though—'

'When I see you, Lisa,' said Antony firmly, and put down the receiver. 'Do *you* think I'm mad, love,' he asked, turning from the phone. 'I'd like to know because I'm beginning to dread having to expound my theories again when I get to Chedcombe.'

'Of course I don't,' Jenny assured him. 'All the same,' she added thoughtfully, 'even supposing one of those men – or another one we haven't even heard of yet – wanted Sandra to be a widow, I don't see how that helps about the baby's death. A rich widow, or at least one in control of her son's fortune until he came of age, would surely be preferable to a penniless one. I know you said jokingly that perhaps he didn't like children, but people with enough money don't have to see much of their offspring if they don't want to, even during the nursery years. And after that—'

'Jenny love, you're showing signs of becoming logical again,' Maitland told her. 'You should fight against the tendency, because I don't know if I can bear it.'

'Come and sit down and drink your sherry then and we won't talk about it any more,' Jenny promised. 'But don't tell me you haven't got some far-fetched idea into your head about that problem as well, because I just wouldn't believe you.'

Friday, 25th July

I

Things went well on Thursday, or it might be more accurate to say went as Maitland expected. His client would have been unlikely to agree with the other way of expressing it. So Antony deputised his clerk, Willett, to phone Lisa to say that he would be arriving in Chedcombe that evening, not so much because he hadn't time to place the call himself but to avoid any further questioning until he could answer face to face. On Friday morning he had a leisurely breakfast and strolled round to the offices of Williams & Traherne, Solicitors and Commissioners for Oaths, in good time for his nine-thirty appointment. Lisa must have been waiting to pounce on him, because she rescued him from the waiting-room within about three seconds of his having been left there.

'I've been thinking and thinking,' she said, as she led him into her own room and closed the door on the outer world. 'Why did Vera suggest that I should have a word with Dr Garfield if the chance arose, and why were you so pleased about it?'

'It's a long story,' said Maitland. That wasn't strictly true, it could be told in a few words, but he was afraid the explanations that followed might prove more troublesome. 'But before we get to that, what evidence did the police bring forward to ensure Henrietta would be committed for trial?'

'Two women who said they saw her at the shopping centre the day the Swift baby was taken away. The trouble is, though this didn't come out, of course, Henrietta doesn't seem to know whether she was there or not. And the doctor who delivered her baby and broke the news to her that it was dead. I don't know how he expected her to take it. He was obviously sympathetic, but . . . I don't care how long a story it is,' said Lisa, obviously

150

not willing to wait any longer. 'Tell me!'

'I'm beginning to wonder whether Walter Linwood might have been murdered as well,' said Maitland baldly.

'But there was never any question . . . Dr Garfield had been attending him regularly, so even though he hadn't been expecting anything of the sort there didn't have to be an inquest. I know this from local gossip, not because the doctor told me himself.'

'Did he happen to mention when Walter was taken ill?'

'In the early hours of the morning following the dinner party, but this isn't from the horse's mouth, it's local gossip too. Sandra told their housekeeper, and the housekeeper told Hilda, and Hilda told someone or other – her boy friend probably, and presently it was all round the village. You know what a delight people take in medical details, so I daresay they got it accurately enough.'

'Just the time he was taken ill?'

'Oh no, all the gruesome details. It seems that Sandra wasn't sleeping very well, and she heard him groaning, and when she turned on the light and asked him what was the matter – they had twin beds – he complained of pain in his chest and when he tried to sit up he said he was dizzy. She tried to take his pulse, but it seemed just as usual, but she called the doctor straight away and when he got there he said she wouldn't have been able to tell by his pulse anyway, only a stethoscope would have revealed the fact that his heart had slowed down to an extraordinary extent. Dr Garfield went downstairs to call the ambulance, and when he got back to the bedroom Walter's heartbeat had become rapid and irregular, and before the ambulance could get there he was dead.'

'There's a substance which can be used in the treatment of heart disease, but which taken in excess would have produced just those symptoms.' Antony had done his homework the evening before.

'That isn't to say it was used. Don't you see, if we try to say Walter was murdered that brings the whole thing right back to Oliver again?'

'That's exactly what Uncle Nick told me, but it isn't what I mean to imply at all.' He went reluctantly into his explanation, just as he had done at home the previous Sunday, and found as he had expected that Lisa had no difficulty at all in coming up with

151

all the objections that his family had already produced.

'I don't see that it helps at all,' she repeated when at last the subject seemed to be exhausted.

'I'm only too ready to agree with you, but I think it's worth trying. I know you said Henrietta didn't seem to care too much what happened to her, but if you're right that was the result of what was more or less a self-imposed imprisonment. Do you think she's likely to enjoy three or four months in Chedcombe gaol before the trial can come on?'

'No, and I don't want Oliver to have to go through. But I don't believe that Walter being murdered – if he really was – would make either of their defences any easier.'

'Not unless . . . I'm afraid you may be right, Lisa, but at least I want to give it a try.' He broke off as a thought struck him. 'You're not thinking I may try to get Henrietta off at Oliver's expense, are you?'

'No, of course not.' Lisa sounded indignant. 'I know you hate people saying they've heard of you, though of course pretty well everyone in Chedcombe and round about has, but I do know enough about you to know I can trust you. Implicitly,' she added, sounding pleased with the word.

'That's almost worse,' said Maitland ruefully. 'You can trust me not to double-cross you, that I grant, but to reach the result we both want . . . that's a different matter.'

'It's good enough for me,' said Lisa. 'You said you didn't want me to come with you to see Marilyn Parker, but is there anything else you'd like me to do?'

'Not for the moment. If I get to the stage where I think it would be worth talking to Chief Inspector Camden I'd like you to come with me. But it's not likely to be a cordial meeting, so if you'd rather keep out of it I shall quite understand.'

'I'll come with you, naturally, but if it's just to tell him what you've been telling me this morning I don't see that it'll do the slightest good.'

'No, we shall need something a little more than that. If I come back here after I've talked to Mrs Parker would you drive me over to Madingley? We could have lunch at the Saracen's Head, and perhaps I might be lucky enough to find Dr Garfield at home and have a word with him myself.'

'If you're going to suggest to him that he signed the death certificate when his patient had really been murdered, I don't think he'll be very pleased to see you,' Lisa pointed out.

'That's probably the understatement of the year,' said Antony, smiling at her rather tentative tone. 'But what I suspect is something any doctor would have accepted in perfectly good faith, and with any luck I can make him realise that.' A sudden thought struck him. 'I say, Walter Linwood wasn't cremated, was he?'

'No, there was no question of that. The Linwoods have a vault in the churchyard at Madingley. I'm not quite sure how the bodies are disposed of inside, but there was no question of his going anywhere else.'

'That's good.'

'I don't see that that helps either, we couldn't get an exhumation order on what we've got.'

'Don't you think so? The first thing you said to me, Lisa, when I suggested that Walter's death might have been murder was that if it was true it would make things much worse for Oliver. And it just occurred to me this morning that if we put it the right way to Camden, he might be prepared to ask for the order himself. I'm afraid it will involve a little deception on our part, possibly appearing rather stupid in not seeing the implications as you did immediately. Could you put up with that?'

'Of course I could if it would do any good. But I don't know about you, Antony, I'm beginning to feel as if I'm walking straight into quicksand, and getting in deeper at every step.'

'Cheer up, Lisa, we'll sink together if we must.'

'All right.' She didn't sound as if she found the prospect particularly appealing. 'Would you like me to take you to Mrs Parker's and drop you there?'

'No, I don't think so. At least I should like it very much, but I think our association must be confined to Oliver's case for the moment. And that's deception too, but at least it gives me a good excuse if anyone accuses me of ignoring professional etiquette in these matters.'

'All right then, I'll try to get on with some work here until you come back. You know where she lives, next door to Henrietta and Minnie – do you know, it's an odd thing but I never got her

153

surname either? – on the right side as you look at the house.'

'Yes, and I've got her address written down somewhere,' said Antony in a pleased tone, producing one of his inevitable envelopes. 'It's no good going down to the street and expecting a cab to come along, is it? Do you mind phoning for me?'

II

Mrs Marilyn Parker – Maitland never discovered her husband's first name and occupation, but on the whole was glad that he was at work that morning – was obviously engaged in her housework when he arrived. He could hear the sound of a vacuum cleaner, and had to knock twice before she heard him and turned the machine off. When she opened the door she gave him a startled look, which intensified when her eyes went past him and took in the taxi waiting at the kerb. Her first words were not exactly encouraging. 'Who are you and what do you want?' she demanded.

'My name's Maitland—' Antony began, but wasn't allowed to finish.

'Oh, that man.' The next words were, he felt, inevitable. 'I've heard of you,' she said, 'but I don't think I want to talk to you.'

'If you'd let me explain.' He was edging forward as he spoke and took a moment to regret the fact that Roger wasn't with him. His friend was much better at this kind of thing than he was, and had in his time obtained entry for both of them to some of the most unlikely places. 'I'm acting for Mr Oliver Linwood, and I've reason to believe that there are things you could tell me that might help his defence.'

'Not for her?' A jerk of her head indicated the house next door, so that he took it she was referring to Henrietta Vaughan.

'I've received no instructions to do so.' That was, after all, the literal truth. 'But it's always possible that I may be able to persuade the jury that both cases are connected.'

'Hoodwink them you mean into giving your chap the benefit of the doubt,' she said. Maitland could have thought of other ways of putting it, but didn't disagree with her. After a moment she backed away from the door with a show of reluctance that might or might not have been genuine. 'You'd better come in then,' she said ungraciously.

She was a good-looking woman, though to Maitland's eye – probably because of his prejudice in Henrietta's favour – she had a mean look. She was neatly but appropriately dressed for the task she had been doing and the neatness was obvious in her surroundings too as she led him into her sitting-room, which was a replica of Minnie's as to size and shape but its complete antithesis in every other way. The furniture was new, and except for a vase of flowers on the table in the corner there was no ornamentation at all. The vacuum cleaner could hardly, he felt, qualify for that description.

'You'll have to excuse the untidiness,' said Marilyn unnecessarily, moving one of the chairs a fraction of an inch from where it had been standing. 'I always like to get things nice for the weekend.'

There was nothing much to be said to that, but Maitland achieved a congratulatory murmur. 'I'm sorry to interrupt you,' he added, 'and I won't keep you long.'

'You'd better not, with that taxi ticking up the minutes outside,' she said, but he thought he detected some signs of a thaw in her manner. 'You'd better sit down as long as you're here and tell me what you want.'

'To ask you about Miss Vaughan's condition when she came back from the hospital after losing her baby. I understand you were a friend of hers.'

'We knew each other,' she amended. 'Living next door like this how could we help it?' She paused a moment and gave him a considering look. 'Did you know she's been arrested?' she asked.

'There was a reference in the local paper this morning to the Magistrates' Court hearing,' said Antony. Again the truth, and again misleading.

'I wondered you see, coming from London and all.'

'I came up from town last night.' She seemed to be waiting for some further explanation but he had a feeling that the less said the better. 'Can you help me I wonder?'

'About Henrietta's condition?' she said musingly. 'I went to see her of course as soon as she got home, and Minnie had the cheek to tell me not to upset her. You'd think no one had lost a baby before, but she'd properly gone to pieces. It may have been along of the kid having no father and being let down like that. Not a nice position for a girl to find herself in, and if she does marry that Eddie it won't be a white wedding. But of course she's not in a position to marry anyone now, is she?'

'Hardly.' He stopped himself in time from adding, more's the pity. This was the tricky part, and he didn't want to say the wrong thing. 'I have heard,' he said carefully, 'that it was you who first suggested to the police that her mental condition might furnish a clue to the two deaths near here.'

'My civic duty,' said Marilyn with dignity.

'Certainly it was if you had any suspicions, but when did the idea first come to you?'

'Not right off, I can tell you that. Well, it's not the kind of thing you think about someone you know, is it? But then when I got the letter—'

'*What letter?*'

She disliked interruptions as much as Sir Nicholas did, and particularly perhaps one made in quite such a vehement tone. 'I'll tell this my own way *if* you don't mind. It was just a letter, typed, not signed, and it said, *If you don't do something about that mad woman next door, who's to say your baby will be safe when it comes?* And it said, *The police ought to know, talk to Dr Elliott at St Luke's hospital if you don't agree with me.*'

'I can see I should have congratulated you, but I didn't know you were expecting a happy event,' said Antony, cringing mentally at the phrase but feeling at the same time that it was the one she was most likely to appreciate.

'Well I don't show yet, do I? It's not till January, you see.'

'May I ask, will you be going to St Luke's?'

'Oh yes, it's the best place and I was born there myself as a matter of fact.'

'Does that kind of thing have to be arranged a long time in advance?'

'It's as well to. They have classes, you see, for expectant mothers and fathers, and we're going to those.'

'I see. So you got this letter, and that made you wonder, I suppose.'

'Well, of course it did. There was Henrietta going about as if she wasn't all there, and there were these two poor babies kidnapped and suffocated. But I didn't quite like to go straight to the police so I did what the letter suggested and went to see Dr Elliott instead.'

'Did you know him before that?'

'When we registered for the course he was there and said a few words before the speaker got started. And I remember as a little girl Mother taking me to watch him and his wife come out of church. A big wedding they had, along of her being an heiress or so Mother said. She was proper upset when she heard of her dying like that not so long after.'

'Were you surprised at being told to consult him?'

'Not really. He spoke ever so nicely that time I told you about, and I thought perhaps someone else who was there had got the idea about Henrietta but didn't want to get involved. Only when I thought about it, it didn't seem like something I could just ignore.'

'And was Dr Elliott able to help you?'

'Well, he didn't like it of course, and he'd a lot to say about people who write anonymous letters. He didn't remember Henrietta's case, I mean it's not his job to know all the patients in the hospital, but he had it looked up, and then he asked me what I thought of her mental state, and at last he said since the suggestion had been made it was only right the police should look into it, so I went straight round from the hospital to the police station and I'm not sorry I went, because I don't suppose they'll send her to prison but somewhere where she'll get proper treatment. But it was a bit worrying when all the talk started, right after the first time the police came here and questioned her.'

'When was that?'

'I got the letter and went to see the doctor and then the police on a Friday, because I remember I had to leave my clean-up. I think it was the fourth of July. And they – the police – must have thought about what I said a bit because the first time they came next door was the following day.'

'You've no doubt in your own mind now, Mrs Parker, as to what happened to those two children?'

'None at all. I don't believe she went over to Madingley though and killed that other baby. The state she was in it would have been too much trouble. So I don't see really how what I can have to say will help this Linwood chap.'

He didn't contradict her. 'Well, we tried,' he said and smiled at her. He was liking her better now, though he still couldn't see how knowing Henrietta she could ever have thought her capable of those first two deaths. 'I won't keep you any longer from your housework, though it doesn't look to me as if there was very much left to be done,' he went on looking round appreciatively. 'But before I go I must thank you for giving me so much of your time, and for your kindness in answering what must have seemed some very tiresome questions.'

And he went back to his taxi. It was a different driver today, not quite so cheerfully willing as his predecessor, but perhaps that was just as well as Maitland was in no mood for conversation. The anonymous letter, of course, would be in the possession of the police, but as far as Camden was concerned it had led him in the right direction, he must feel, and that was its only importance.

Lisa was waiting for him and took him straight out to where her car was parked. But she seemed to sense his mood and didn't worry him with questions as they drove back to Madingley, and even while they ate a ploughman's lunch at the Saracen's Head she was unwontedly quiet. Only when they parted later outside Dr Garfield's house did she break her self-imposed silence. 'I'm not going back to the office,' she said, 'it isn't worth it on Friday afternoon. So you can come straight back to the cottage when you're through here.'

'And you'll take me to see Inspector Camden, if we can get hold of him that is?'

Suddenly Lisa grinned impishly. 'If that's your idea of a pleasant afternoon,' she said, 'I'll take you with pleasure.'

III

If he hadn't already done so, as soon as he saw Mrs Garfield Maitland would have deleted her husband's name from his list of suspects. She was a plump, smiling woman, obviously one of those on whom the slings and arrows of fortune have very little effect. 'You're lucky, Mr Maitland,' she said after he had introduced himself. 'Bob's in the garden, and nobody's expecting a baby, or dying at the moment, so you'll probably be able to talk as long as you like.' She led him through the house into a garden that was larger than he had expected, and obviously lovingly tended, though at the moment the doctor, in slacks, a short-sleeved shirt, and a disgraceful hat, was dealing out death and destruction among his roses with a formidable-looking spray.

He was a little shorter than his wife and a good deal slimmer, and when he had led the way to chairs in the shade and took off the hat it was obvious why he had worn it as a protection from the sun, as he was completely bald. 'It's odd,' said Maitland, seating himself, 'you don't seem at all surprised to see me, Doctor.'

'One of the things you must realise,' said Dr Garfield, 'is that nothing that goes on in a country place like this is ever a secret.'

'I know that, but—'

'So when Lisa Traherne came to see me with some rather odd questions to ask it was only natural that I wondered how long you would be behind her.'

It was obviously no good beating about the bush with this man. 'You've guessed then, Doctor, what is troubling me?'

'You're wondering if Walter Linwood was murdered as well as his son,' said Garfield calmly. 'I'm pretty sure you're wrong, you know, but in your place I can see I might have a few doubts.'

'I'll try not to ask you any questions that you might feel improper to answer, but do you mind talking a little about the evening before his death?'

'I've done so already, to Lisa.'

'Yes, but . . . I'll be honest with you, doctor.' He broke off there and added rather ruefully, 'And if anyone said that to me I'd suspect his motives from the start.'

'I'm willing to accept your assurance,' said Garfield solemnly, 'that your motives are of the purest.'

'Thank you. Let me begin by saying that I can quite see that if what I suspect really happened you would have had no reason to hesitate in signing the death certificate. It's probably impertinent as a layman for me to say so, but I don't want you to think I'm

159

trying to stir up trouble.'

'I think my reputation in these parts is reasonably secure,' said Garfield placidly. 'What exactly is in your mind, Mr Maitland?'

'Digitoxin perhaps. One of the glycocides of Digitalis at any rate.'

'You obviously know something about the subject.'

'I had a case once in which it was involved, otherwise I'm afraid I'm very ignorant on medical matters. Supposing such a thing had been administered—'

'It would have produced precisely the symptoms that Sandra described to me when she called me out in the early hours of the following morning. I may add, in answer to what I think is going to be your next question, that nothing I ever prescribed for Walter Linwood could have had a cumulative effect of that kind.'

'I'm sure of that, but at least it means that if any traces are found we can prove—'

'You're going a bit too quickly for me, Mr Maitland. What have you in mind?'

'Can't you guess that too, Doctor? You seem to me to have a very good understanding.'

'You seem to be suggesting that we should apply for an exhumation order. Do you think the coroner would agree to that?'

'If the police will back me up, and if you don't put a spoke in my wheel by insisting that the death couldn't possibly have been anything but natural . . . he might.'

'I wouldn't do that.' He paused and gave his companion a long, inquiring look. 'I can see, Mr Maitland, that you wouldn't have made this suggestion frivolously, so I'm willing to give you what help I can. But I've two questions first. Exactly what help would it be to Oliver's defence if you proved that his cousin was murdered? And how are you going to persuade Chief Inspector Camden that the idea is a reasonable one?'

Antony smiled at him. 'I've a very good excuse for not answering the first part of that question,' he said. 'It directly concerns a case I'm involved in for the defence, whereas you're a witness for the prosecution. But unless and until Walter Linwood's death is proved to be murder there's no reason whatever why we shouldn't discuss it as much as we like.'

'That seems rather specious reasoning,' said the doctor,

amused. 'It leaves open the second question, however.'

'My old friend Inspector Camden? You put your finger on it very neatly when you said that proving Walter was murdered wouldn't help Oliver. On the face of it that's true, but if I can persuade Camden that I haven't realised the fact he might be willing to back me up . . . don't you think? You see if I'm proved wrong . . . well I'll look a bit of a fool, but that's not going to trouble him. Whereas if I'm right the case against my client, as he sees it, will be considerably strengthened.'

'But you don't think so?'

'It's a chance I've got to take, because I have to admit to you, doctor, that I don't see any way of proving Oliver's innocence except by proving someone else's guilt. I've explained why I can't discuss it with you, but some day I will, I promise you that. Because you've been far more kind and generous than I had any right to expect.'

Dr Garfield waved that aside. 'Is there any other way I can help you?'

'One question. If by any chance I'm right, when would the fatal dose have had to be given?'

'That's impossible to say exactly without a post mortem. It would depend on how much had actually been ingested. Though death at the last is apt to come quite suddenly, as is the case with natural heart failure, the reaction would be by no means immediate. So until we know more you would have to look at a period from say nine o'clock in the evening on.' He paused again and gave Antony another of his penetrating looks. 'I must say, Mr Maitland, you're a somewhat disconcerting companion.'

'I'm sorry about that.'

'Well, to save you the embarrassment of yet another question I'll tell you without your asking that I saw and heard nothing during that evening to suggest that matters were not completely normal. Looking back I can't believe you're right in your suspicion, but I realise you're completely sincere about this and as I said I'll put no obstacle in your way. But I hope you're wrong, because I can't for the life of me see that anyone would benefit from both Walter's death and his son's except Oliver and – perhaps this is something else that it's improper for me to say to you – I simply can't believe it of him.'

161

'Hold on to that thought, Doctor, and keep your fingers crossed for me when I talk to Camden,' said Antony getting up. 'I can tell you,' he added as the doctor walked beside him round the side of the house towards the front gate, 'that's not an interview I'm looking forward to with much pleasure. However, who lives may learn, and at least Lisa Traherne has promised to hold my coat.'

IV

Maitland walked back to the Trahernes' cottage and found Dominic, still in his work clothes, taking tea with his wife in the garden. Lisa said, 'Camden?' inquiringly, and got up without a word when Antony nodded. Dominic poured him tea, and didn't attempt to question him, and he had barely had time to take his first sip when Lisa came back.

'He's free and will see us if we go over right away,' she said. 'I had to do a bit of fast talking to persuade him there'd be no impropriety involved in a discussion between us, but I did my best to sound a bit fluttery – that was what you wanted, wasn't it? – so he probably thinks we're somewhere on the edge of despair.'

Antony nearly said, Aren't we? but forbore out of consideration for her feelings. His talk with Marilyn Parker had gone a long way towards convincing him of the rightness of his theory, but his talk with Dr Garfield, pleasant thought it had been, had gone even further towards convincing him of the difficulty of the course he was embarked on. 'All we're going to do, Lisa,' he said, 'is to try to get his co-operation in applying to the coroner for an exhumation order for Walter Linwood. You know yourself the first thing that comes to everyone's mind when I say he may have been murdered, but it's absolutely essential that we convince the Chief Inspector, one way or another, that that very evident conclusion has occurred to neither of us. If we can do that he may agree, either in the hope of seeing me made a fool of, or in the hope of strengthening the case against Oliver. Do you think we can convince him that we're both clutching at straws, and a bit stupid into the bargain?'

'You obviously realise,' said Dominic, who had been listening

162

with some interest, 'that everybody in this neighbourhood knows a good deal about your doings in the past. Don't you think Camden, more than anybody else, knows that you're not likely to be quite so silly? I'm quite sure Lisa can play the scatterbrain if she wants to, acting seems to come naturally to women,' (Lisa pulled a face at him) 'but I'm not so sure about you.'

'People will tell you there's a good deal of the actor in most barristers,' Antony told him, 'and I'm a fair mimic myself when I set my mind to it.' Which was something of an understatement, it had always been one of his strongest abilities and probably accounted for the facility with which he had always picked up foreign languages. 'And what you have to remember, Dominic, is that if we play it right he'll *want* to believe us for the reasons I just gave, which is more than half the battle. So I think we have to try.'

'I'll go and get the car,' said Lisa, and without taking her eyes from the road or causing him undue alarm in any other way chattered nineteen to the dozen all the way into Chedcombe, until his head was reeling.

'You'll do,' he told her as she brought the car to a halt in the parking area behind the police station. 'I think perhaps I'd better let you do most of the talking.'

'All right, what shall I say?'

'Dr Garfield admits there was nothing inconsistent in Walter's death with his having taken a toxic dose of one of the digitalis derivatives. They're called glycocides, can you remember that?'

'Yes, I think so.'

'He also says he never gave Walter any medicine containing Digitoxin, which is the most common form, so that if it is found it will create a strong presumption that someone gave it to him deliberately, knowing of his heart condition. You can be a bit vaguer than Dr Garfield was about the time it might have been administered, though it's quite true he said there was no telling until the exact amount remaining in the body was known. Give Camden the impression, if you like, that I'm the sort of person who sees a murderer behind every bush, I'll give you what help about that that I can. You needn't even agree with me, perhaps you're just humouring me, but don't for a minute let him see that you realise that if Walter's death was a preliminary to the baby's murder it could create an even stronger impression of Oliver's guilt.'

'Yes,' said Lisa rather doubtfully, 'I think I can do that. But you will put a word in if I seem to be drying up, won't you?'

'Trust me,' said Maitland. 'Let me start the ball rolling, if I can succeed in reminding him how much he dislikes me, he may be all the more ready to agree to a course of action so obviously to my disadvantage.'

They got out of the car then. 'Why does he dislike you?' said Lisa as she came round the car.

'He doesn't like interference in what he considers is solely his business,' said Antony. 'And altogether I don't know that I blame him,' he added meditatively, 'but all the same we can't have him going around arresting innocent people.'

They got back to Madingley not much more than an hour later to find Dominic already bathed and changed, having succumbed to temptation and knocked off early. He was standing in the kitchen regarding the stew Mrs Biggins had left for them with a rather jaundiced eye. 'If only she had some imagination,' he said mournfully and turned to greet them, obviously bursting with questions but refraining with true nobility from asking them.

'I really came back so that we could talk privately,' said Antony, 'but after that I think it would be a very good idea if you and Lisa came and had dinner with me at the hotel.'

'We'd like to, of course. That thing,' said Dominic with loathing – he seemed to have taken a particular dislike to that evening's offering – 'can go into the freezer until Monday. Thank heaven we cook for ourselves at the weekends. Though if we can be seen dining together I don't quite see why you couldn't have stayed here.'

'There is a difference. Your presence, my dear Dominic,' said Maitland, growing, had his listeners only realised it, more like Sir Nicholas at every moment, 'will lend respectability to the occasion ... professionally, I mean. In any event, to dine together in public is far less compromising than for me to accept your hospitality here.'

'All right then, we'll have a drink while we talk,' said Dominic following the others into the living-room and starting to rummage immediately in the cupboard where the various ingredients were

164

housed. 'But why so stuffy all of a sudden?' he asked, not looking round from his task. 'Does that mean that Inspector Camden turned you down flat?'

'Far from it. Tell him, Lisa,' said Antony, sinking down into the chair he had adopted as his own on his previous visit.

'We were both marvellous,' said Lisa, obviously seeing no reason for false modesty. 'You should have been there, Dominic, you'd have been willing to bet that we'd both been on the stage for years. Of course, that wasn't what Chief Inspector Camden thought, he thought every word we said was perfectly genuine.'

'In a way, Lisa, it was, the truth but not the whole truth,' said Antony accepting a glass of sherry and mentally commending his host for having a good memory.

'Well, I suppose that's right. Come to think of it we didn't tell any lies, we just conveyed a wrong impression. You'd have been proud of us, Dominic. First of all Antony set out to rile poor Inspector Camden—'

'Poor my foot!' said Maitland under his breath.

'—telling him about all the inquiries he'd been making; and the conclusion they led him to that Walter Linwood had been murdered as well. You know what they say about a red rag to a bull, that was just the effect it had on Camden. So when I started wittering on about applying for an exhumation order he fell for it like a ton of bricks. From his point of view it doesn't matter a scrap whether we find Walter was poisoned or not; if he was everything would look blacker still for Oliver, and if he wasn't Antony's reputation for infallibility would have gone for a burton.'

'Good heaven's, Lisa, where on earth did you pick up that bit of old-fashioned slang?'

'From Dad I expect. You seem to know what it means anyway.'

'That's rather different.'

'The man who never loses a case,' said Dominic thoughtfully, ignoring that last exchange.

'Yes it was in Chedcombe that stupid phrase was coined,' Antony agreed. 'I've said a thousand times, I only wish it were true. Anyway, by the time Lisa had finished with him Camden didn't know whether he was coming or going, and the result was he agreed like a lamb to talk to the coroner.'

'I didn't see anything particularly lamb-like about him,' said Lisa. 'I thought he was hating your guts,' she added crudely.

'That was the whole point of the exercise . . . but never mind that. We still don't know whether the coroner will play ball or not. Or if he does how long will getting the results take?'

'Not long,' said Lisa confidently.

'You sound as if you'd attended an exhumation every other week since you qualified.'

'No, I've never attended one at all actually, but I have read about them in books.'

'Well, we'll hope for the best. I'll go back to town tomorrow, but come back straight away when you give me the word.'

'It's getting very near the end of the Trinity Term,' Lisa reminded him.

'Yes, but Jenny and I always visit a very old friend during the vacation. He'll understand quite well if we're a few days late.'

'All right then, I'll keep an eye on things here. But meanwhile . . . you've come to some conclusion, Antony. I mean I can quite see someone might have wanted to murder Walter, to leave Sandra free to marry again. But the motive for the babies' deaths—'

'You'll have to forgive me, both of you, if I start with the bare assumption that Oliver is innocent,' said Maitland. 'After all, it was you two who insisted on that from the beginning.'

'I didn't think you were sure though.'

'I wasn't until today, nearly sure but not quite.'

'What convinced you?'

'My talk with Marilyn Parker. But I'll come to that in a moment. You've also got to accept on my word that Henrietta didn't kill those other two babies either. Camden will maintain, and it's not an altogether ridiculous assumption, that their deaths gave Oliver the idea of killing his own cousin and getting her blamed for it. But two people going around the place smothering babies is just one too many for me. I think all the deaths were connected, and at this point I'm damned sure we'll find that Walter was poisoned too.'

Dominic had finished mixing the rather more complicated drinks that he and Lisa favoured and now came to join the others.

'I'm quite willing, Antony, and I'm sure Lisa is, to take those two facts for granted ... Oliver's innocence and the innocence of Henrietta Vaughan. But you've still got a lot of explaining to do unless you want us both to die of curiosity. Where do we go from here?'

'To a description of my state of mind before I came back from London,' Maitland told him.

'You'd obviously come to the conclusion that Walter had been murdered,' Dominic prompted him.

'Yes, because I was trying to make some sense out of the fact you both seemed to be so sure of, that Oliver wasn't guilty. And after a while I began to get the glimmering of an idea. It seemed to be generally accepted that Sandra wouldn't be altogether inconsolable in her widowhood, however little she desired her husband's death at the time. If someone had wanted her to be free to marry again, then Walter's death was obviously the first move in the game. Taking that as a starting point one had to assume that there was also some motive for the Linwood baby's death, and I came to the conclusion that the other two had been killed as a camouflage to make it seem that there was a lunatic at large. I admit at that point the reason for the Linwood baby's death escaped me completely, but if Oliver was innocent there had to be some explanation of that. And if either of you tell me all this was pure guesswork I shall probably shake the dust of this cottage from my shoes forever and walk back to Chedcombe. I've heard quite enough on those lines from my loving family, and particularly from my uncle.'

'Are he and Vera really happy together?' asked Lisa inconsequently.

'And I was beginning to think that I'd found that *rara avis*, a woman whose mind was not first concerned with personalities,' said Antony, amused by the question. 'The answer is that I've never seen a happier couple, present company excepted of course and not stressing the fact, as Vera may have told you, that I have the best wife in the world.'

'Well,' said Dominic, anxious to keep him to the point, though if he had but known it wasn't in the slightest degree necessary, 'we'll agree if you like that all this was perfectly logical, so what was your next conclusion?'

'Let's see, we'd just got Walter killed off, hadn't we? So the next thing was to decide who might have had designs on Sandra.'

'You've quite abandoned the idea that someone might have had a grudge against her?' asked Lisa. 'Jean Colborne—'

'Yes, she's spiteful enough,' said Maitland without waiting for her to finish. 'But I don't think she'd have been the type to concoct such an elaborate plot. We're still working on the assumption that all three children were killed by the same person, remember. Besides there are reasons . . . I'll come to those in a moment. And for those same reasons . . . plus one other, I crossed both the Blunts off the list. It's a horrible thing to say about anybody, but I don't think they cared whether that unfortunate child lived or died. But they could have got rid of it quite easily if they'd wanted to, without indulging in such an elaborate scheme.'

'Yes, I'll grant you that,' said Lisa, sounding rather startled.

'So that brings us back to the men who might have wanted to see Sandra a widow. Jean Colborne certainly thought her husband was one of them, but Walter's death wouldn't have been much use to him without his wife's too, and I'm quite sure he's too intelligent a man not to realise there'd be a few eyebrows raised if she died suddenly as well. I've heard one or two hints that your friend Mr Weatherby was fond of her—'

'That's nonsense,' said Lisa bluntly, ready, as ever, to come to the defence of her friends.

'Bear with me. There is also Dr Clifford Elliott, who dined at Linwood House the night before Walter died.'

'But he'd been a friend of Walter's for ages,' Lisa protested.

'If he fell really hard for Sandra I don't think that would make any difference. This is where we come to the point I spoke to you about, consideration of which, to my mind, leads directly to him. Marilyn Parker, if you remember, consulted him before she went to the police with her suspicions about Henrietta.'

'But in the circumstances he couldn't have given her any other advice than to let the police look into the matter.'

'Yes, Lisa, but when I went to see Mrs Parker this morning she told me something that confirmed the suspicions I already had, that clinched the matter as far as I'm concerned. She had an anonymous letter, rather a cruel one really, accusing Henrietta, and advising her to talk to Dr Elliott at the hospital if she was in any doubt about what to do.'

'How do you mean, cruel?' asked Dominic.

'She's expecting a baby, just about the same time as Lisa's will arrive. The note intimated that it might go the same way as the others if Henrietta wasn't put away.'

'Yes I see. Was that the first time she'd thought about the possibility of Henrietta's guilt?'

'She'd been a bit impatient with her for mooning about as she put it, and not snapping out of it as quickly as Marilyn thought she should. At least that's the impression she gave me, but once she'd read the letter it all got exaggerated in her mind, and she began to think that after all Henrietta had had two blows, losing her baby and being deserted by its father, whose name, I've just realised, I've yet to learn. By the way, I didn't know you had that tradition in your part of the world too.'

'What tradition?'

'I've only heard of it in Yorkshire, and even there I think it's dying out. A girl who "has to get married", as the saying is, or still worse who's had an illegitimate baby, wears blue to her wedding instead of white. I can't imagine why, because if the baby hasn't arrived yet it's just advertising the fact to the world.'

'Yes, they do that here too,' said Dominic. 'At least they do in the country, but as you say it's not quite so faithfully observed nowadays.'

'In Chedcombe, too,' said Lisa. 'I always thought it was a sort of superstition.'

'You may be right.' Maitland, who always returned to his theme however far he might have deviated from it, took up his explanation where he had left off. 'You do see what that means, don't you? It means there was a deliberate attempt to frame Henrietta for the murders and once you get to that point the next step is obvious. Of all the people we've been talking about, Dr Clifford Elliott is the only one who knew she'd lost her own baby and been a little more than usually upset by the fact. What's more, he pretended to Mrs Parker that he didn't remember her and had to have the matter looked up. An added bonus, of course, is that he was in a position to find out, without arousing anybody's suspicions, what new babies were around. And when it came to killing Walter, obviously he was able to get hold of anything toxic that he wanted, as well as having the knowledge to give him something that made the death appear natural. You can distil the stuff I'm supposing was used – and that's another guess – from the common foxglove, but I imagine it's a messy business, and I can't somehow visualise Mr Weatherby undertaking it, crouched over his kitchen stove.'

'That's a relief anyway,' said Lisa. 'But, good heavens, you're giving us an awful lot to think about. If Walter was really murdered to leave Sandra free to marry again, and if for some reason the poor little baby was in the way . . . well, the murderer had got away with Walter's death without arousing any suspicion, so why not let Oliver take the blame for killing little Mark?'

'Because no one could have known he'd be visiting Linwood House at that particular moment. He might have been at the Saracen's Head, and had an unbreakable alibi.'

'Yes, that's true.' Lisa was still speaking slowly and obviously thinking the matter through as she did so. 'Are you saying that Dr Elliott was of such a jealous disposition that he couldn't bear to share Sandra with another man's child?'

'That's possible, of course, I don't know him well enough to say. But Marilyn Parker told me another thing, she said her mother had taken her when she was a child to watch the doctor and his bride leaving the church, it had been a big wedding because the new Mrs Elliott was an heiress, and Marilyn's mother – who seems to have been rather a connoisseur of weddings – was quite upset when she died a few years later.'

'You're not saying she was murdered too?'

'Nothing of the sort. We've got quite enough on our plate as it is. What I am pointing out is that there was no lack of money, Sandra would have had the use of her child's fortune until he came of age, but the doctor didn't have to consider that when he wanted to marry again.'

'It's getting worse and worse.' said Lisa in a tragic tone. 'But it still doesn't explain—'

'I don't know how devoted Sandra was to her husband, but as they'd only been married two years I don't suppose the glamour had entirely worn off. It's been suggested that she would consider marrying again, and for her sake I hope that's true because she's very young to spend the rest of her life alone. But what no-one seems to be in any doubt about is that there was a mercenary streak in her nature. Don't marry for money, in other words, but marry where money is.'

'He wanted her penniless so that she'd turn to him.' Lisa still sounded incredulous. 'Antony, you may be right, Vera says you have a knack of it, but how on earth do you think you're going to get anyone to believe all this?'

'It seems reasonable enough to me,' said Dominic, 'I've known Sandra for a long time, even though it wasn't very well. If she were independent financially she might think the doctor was too old for her, he must be eight or nine years older than Walter at least. But with Oliver inheriting she'd certainly be looking for a new meal ticket.'

'What a very vulgar way of putting it,' Lisa rebuked him. 'But . . . he was very positive about Oliver's innocence when we talked to him, wasn't he, Antony? Supposing you're right about all this, supposing the exhumation order is granted and proves that Walter was murdered, what do you mean to do then?'

'Point out to Camden that his case against Henrietta has melted away, giving him as little information as I can in the process. Oliver . . . I don't think it's going to drive Oliver mad to spend the summer in prison, people say his ways are odd but to me he seems an extraordinarily well-balanced person. And when the case comes on . . . I can't say anything better or more hopeful than wait and see. I shall talk to Dera Mohamad again and perhaps to some of the other nurses, and if I find that Dr Elliott has been taking an undue interest in the maternity ward . . . I can't promise anything, I wish I could.'

'No, of course not. You'll do your best,' said Lisa, and wondered at the sudden shadow that passed across Maitland's face, almost as though he were in pain. 'We'll do our best,' she amended.

'Does that mean you're with me?'

'All the way!' said Lisa buoyantly. And added unwittingly another phrase that Maitland particularly disliked. 'If anyone can get Oliver off . . . we're trusting you,' she said.

Their dinner at the George passed pleasantly enough, with no more talk of legal matters. But after that it wasn't surprising that Antony slept badly.

Saturday, 26th July

The best train on Saturday didn't leave until just past noon. Maitland had tea and the local newspaper in his room, and went down late to breakfast, intending to dawdle over the meal. He had phoned Jenny the previous evening giving her his time of arrival, and was quite prepared to find his whole family assembled to greet him when he finally got home.

But nothing, as he should have known, ever comes quite up to expectations. He had finished his kipper, poured his second cup of coffee, and was reaching for the marmalade when he became aware of a presence beside him. He looked up and saw a slim woman, a little over middle height, wearing a grey chiffon dress just a little too elegant for a summer morning in a country town, and with fair hair that looked as if it and she had come straight from the ministrations of her hairdresser. At first glance he realised she was uncommonly good-looking, the fact that she was also very angry took a moment or two more to sink in.

'The waiter says you're the man who's acting for my cousin,' she said, without any preliminary greeting.

Antony scrambled to his feet. 'I imagine he told you my name is Maitland,' he replied. 'And, yes, I am Oliver Linwood's counsel. From the way you refer to him I gather you must be Mrs Sandra Linwood.'

'Of course I am!'

'In that case I must offer you my sincere condolences for the loss of your husband, and then, so soon after, the death of your baby. I should have called on you for that purpose if it hadn't been for the convention that forbids me to talk to anyone who may appear for the prosecution when my client is tried.' He was struggling desperately to reduce the situation to normality, she'd

173

be breathing fire at any moment. 'Perhaps you weren't aware of this, but we shouldn't be talking together.'

'I don't want to talk to you about Oliver, if that's what you mean.'

'In that case, won't you sit down and I'll send for some more coffee.' The waiter was hovering, obviously listening to every word, and Maitland caught his eye and tapped the lid of the coffee pot, which he hoped would be sufficient to get the man out of the way for the moment. He moved a little to pull out a chair. 'Then you can tell me just what's on your mind,' he invited.

'I should have thought you knew perfectly well.' She glared at him for a moment and then sat down as though with reluctance. 'This ridiculous suggestion about my husband.'

'Chief Inspector Camden has been to see you,' Maitland hazarded.

'He very properly told me what was in the wind, and he also told me that the idea was yours. I don't believe it for a moment, that Walter was killed I mean, and I won't have it!'

'It was, as you say, very proper that the Inspector should inform you of what was proposed,' Antony agreed. 'And I can understand that the idea is an unpleasant one for you. But it will be up to the coroner, you know. It's out of my hands now.'

'If the police are in favour of it . . . I don't understand, I really don't understand. Chief Inspector Camden seemed to think it was a good idea. He seems to be of the opinion, if it turns out you're right, that it would clinch the case against Oliver.'

The waiter came back at that point with a clean cup and a fresh pot of coffee. Antony poured it for her, but as soon as the man had gone returned as was his custom to the exact point where they had left off. 'Wouldn't that please you?' he asked. This was dangerously close to forbidden ground, but he thought he could get away with the excuse that they were discussing the possibility of Walter's murder, nothing to do with the case against Oliver at this point.

'I don't know, I just don't know.' For the first time anger seemed to be giving way to a genuine distress. 'Oliver's a strange person, I don't understand him. Walter always said live and let live, and let him be happy in his own way. I don't want him to be guilty, though I thought at first he must be. But Cliff says it was

174

obviously that girl in Chedcombe who did it, the one who killed the other babies.'

Fortunately by this time the dining-room had emptied except for themselves, and the waiter was hovering by the door, well out of earshot. 'You mean Dr Clifford Elliott?' Maitland asked, though he knew the answer perfectly well.

'Of course I do. I phoned him to tell him what the Chief Inspector said and that I was coming to—to—'

'Confront me,' Antony suggested, when she seemed to be at a loss for words.

'Well I think it's a horrible idea, and I expect Cliff will be here quite soon to back me up. He quite agreed with me, and said I should do my best to put a stop to the whole thing.'

'Dr Elliott knows as well as I do that it's up to the coroner,' Antony pointed out. 'Of course it's obvious that the authorities would prefer to proceed with your permission—'

'I don't see why *you* should want it, you in particular, if it's going to harm Oliver when you're supposed to be helping him. I've heard enough about you to know you're not a stupid man, Mr Maitland, but the Chief Inspector seemed to think you just hadn't noticed that possibility.'

'My duty is to the court,' said Antony, 'and the court's business is to find out the truth.' As he spoke he realised that the words sounded extraordinarily sententious, but just at the moment he couldn't decide how best to play the scene. If Dr Elliott was also going to show up that might be turned to advantage, but how this might be done was another matter. And just at that moment, the doctor, as though summoned by his thought, appeared in the doorway, looked round for a moment, and started across the room towards them.

'I came as soon as I could, my dear,' he said to Sandra, and seated himself beside her, across the table from Antony. 'Don't you think Mrs Linwood has suffered enough, Mr Maitland?' he asked. His tone was cold, but Antony thought there was some anger there being held in check with difficulty.

'I do and I'm sorry for it,' said Antony sincerely.

'Then put a stop to this nonsense!'

'I'm afraid the matter's out of my hands,' Maitland repeated. 'Once Chief Inspector Camden gets an idea into his head—'

175

'Why the devil did you put it there, you of all people, when you must have seen that if there was any truth in the idea it would harm your client?'

'I don't think that necessarily follows,' said Antony slowly. 'You seem very upset, doctor, over an idea that you categorised as nonsense. If the coroner does agree to grant an exhumation order, what do you think the pathologist will find?'

'Why, nothing, of course.'

'In that case I can see no reason why you should be upset.'

'I'm only thinking of Sandra, of Mrs Linwood.'

The waiter appeared silently at Dr Elliott's elbow and produced yet another pot of coffee. Maitland's own drink was cold, but he sipped it deliberately for a moment, partly waiting until they were alone again and partly to introduce an element of surprise, he hoped, into his next remark. Raising his eyes suddenly he asked directly, 'You're in love with her, aren't you?'

'What an extraordinary question!' Elliott glanced uncertainly at Sandra and added less forcefully, 'Mrs Linwood has been a widow for less than two months, it's hardly time to be speaking of things like that.'

'You haven't denied it,' Antony pointed out.

Sandra was looking from one to the other of her companions in rather a puzzled way. It came to Maitland suddenly that now that her anger had cooled she was a woman capable of very clear thought. Finally her eyes came to rest on Dr Elliott. 'You told me you'd look after me, Cliff,' she said gently.

'As a friend of Walter's . . . don't you realise, my dear, you'll be penniless if Oliver goes free. And Mr Maitland is, as we know, an exceptionally successful advocate.'

'I don't think it's because you were Walter's friend at all,' said Sandra, 'and I'm beginning to wonder—'

'What are you wondering, Mrs Linwood?' Maitland asked when she hesitated.

'If you're right that Walter was poisoned, in some way that deceived Dr Garfield—'

'If he was it was in a way that would have deceived any doctor knowing of your husband's heart condition,' Antony assured her.

'Yes, but that isn't the point. What I was going to ask you, Mr Maitland, was: if that's what happened what are you going to say about it when Oliver comes to trial?'

'Not, I assure you, that it was the first step towards Oliver inheriting,' Antony replied. 'I think it was done to leave you free to marry again.'

'But we'd only been married two years!'

'I know, and I'm sorry to make you think of all these unhappy things. But you're very young, and I'm sure your husband wouldn't have wanted you to spend the rest of your life alone.'

'But poor little Mark?'

'If he had lived you'd have had no financial reason to marry, at least until he came of age, and probably not even then if he was a normal, loving son.'

Sandra closed her eyes, as though the world had suddenly become too difficult a place to look upon. 'I can't believe it,' she said.

'Let's think of something else for the moment then. Henrietta Vaughan.'

'The girl who killed the babies in Chedcombe?'

'The girl who was framed for their murder, in the hope that she would be blamed for what happened to Mark too. Except for the accident of Oliver being present when your baby died that is certainly what would have been believed. Oliver would have inherited, and you would have been penniless.'

'You're going too far and upsetting Mrs Linwood, Mr Maitland,' said Elliott harshly.

'No, I want to hear,' Sandra insisted. 'You say someone deliberately tried to throw the blame on this girl?'

'Yes, I'm sure of it. The idea of her guilt reached the police in a roundabout way, starting with an anonymous letter to a neighbour. The writer of that letter knew that the person it was addressed to was attending pre-natal classes at St Luke's Hospital, he also knew of Henrietta's distress over the death of her own baby.'

'This has gone far enough!' Dr Elliott's chair toppled over backwards as he came to his feet. 'You're getting dangerously near to libel, Mr Maitland.'

'Slander,' Antony corrected automatically. 'But the defence of truth, I must point out to you, is a good one if it can be proved. You do see where all this leads then, doctor,' he said, with the

177

gentleness that mimicked Sir Nicholas's at times, but in this case was a danger signal of a very different sort.

'I— I—'

'Pick up your chair and sit down again, doctor.' To Maitland's relief the waiter had decided some time since that his services were no longer required and had disappeared kitchenwards. He turned back to Sandra again. 'Will you answer one question for me, Mrs Linwood?'

'If I can.' She wasn't looking at Elliott, her eyes were fixed on Maitland's face with painful intensity.

'I'm afraid it's an impertinent one, but believe me the answer's important, not only to Oliver but also in the long run perhaps to you.'

'I've said I'll answer you.'

'Well then, if Dr Elliott had proposed to you, as I gather he's come near to suggesting he would when a suitable time had elapsed, what would have been your reply?'

'I don't want to marry anyone.' There could be no doubt of Sandra's sincerity. 'Can't you understand that I was in love with Walter?'

'Yes, I understand that.' Maitland's tone was gentle, but now in a different way. 'However there's the future to consider, no matter how bleak it may seem at the moment. How will you live if Oliver goes free?'

'I suppose then . . . if Cliff asked me . . . I've never had to earn a living, Mr Maitland, I don't know what else I could do but accept him.'

'I'm sorry to press the matter, Mrs Linwood, but for both our sakes we should get it clear. If such a proposal were made, and financial considerations didn't enter into the equation, how then would you answer?'

'No! I liked him as Walter's friend but I never loved him and I never could.' For the first time since she had addressed him directly she turned her eyes on Elliott, who had obeyed Maitland's injunction so far as to right his chair but was still standing. 'I thought . . . someone older who could advise me,' she said. 'But I don't have to rely on you, Cliff, whatever happens. Mr Byron explained to me what would happen if Oliver is convicted, I should certainly be looked after; and Oliver wrote to me from prison saying he didn't want the house or the income to keep it up and I just don't believe he did that to make it sound better for him at his trial.'

There was a long moment's silence. Clifford Elliott was gripping the back of his chair as if it were a lifeline, but gradually his hold relaxed. He turned on Maitland a look full of hatred, but then his eyes sought Sandra's face, and his expression softened. 'I loved you, my dear, from the first moment I saw you,' he said. 'You must always remember that.' And as he finished speaking he turned on his heel and left them.

All of a sudden Sandra was crying, with an abandon that made Maitland wonder whether she had been able to weep before. And just at that moment the waiter chose to re-appear, probably in hopes that they had finished their discussion and he would be able to clear the table. Maitland dismissed him to fetch a glass of water, and set himself to comfort the girl. 'Do you really mean he killed them both?' she asked him presently, between sobs.

'The babies in Chedcombe as well. But you came to that conclusion – didn't you? – before ever I hammered the fact home to you.'

Sandra gulped, and at last accepted his offer of a handkerchief. 'You'd only to look at his face,' she said, 'and then I remembered, of course, how different his manner had been after Walter was dead. I just felt then that he was being kind, but now I feel as if everything that's happened has been my fault.'

Antony, only too familiar with this frame of mind, thought it had better be dealt with without delay. 'You were in love with your husband,' he said. 'That must have been obvious to everyone who knew you intimately. Therefore he could have gained no encouragement from your manner and trying to accept the blame is just self-indulgence.'

She managed a watery smile at that. 'You must think me awful, Mr Maitland, admitting I'd have married for money. But I could see then what must have been in his mind, and what was in your mind too. What do we do now?'

'Perhaps you should tidy up a bit,' Antony suggested, 'while I phone my wife and tell her I shan't be catching the train I expected to. Then I think we should go together and confess our sins to Chief Inspector Camden. He'll think it all wrong for us to

179

have talked together at all pending Oliver's trial,' he explained when she looked at him inquiringly. 'But perhaps you'll be able to help me to pacify him.'

How far this plan would have been successful he was never to know. Before they had been half an hour at the police station, and while the going was still decidedly sticky, a report came in that Dr Elliott had been found dead in his office at the hospital. The poison was so far unknown, probably one of the quick-acting barbiturates, but he had left a letter addressed to the coroner.

Sunday, 27th July

Maitland got home the following afternoon to find Sir Nicholas and Vera taking tea with Jenny, as he would have expected even if he hadn't known they wanted to hear what he had to say. Jenny came out into the hall to greet him and said, 'Look out for squalls,' in a low tone, even before he had time to kiss her. There was no need to ask what she meant, and he followed her back into the living-room with no outward sign of trepidation.

Sir Nicholas set down his cup. 'I might have known it,' he said tragically. 'For all your protestations you had, I must suppose, no intention of letting either of your clients come to trial.'

'Henrietta Vaughan wasn't my client, Uncle Nick,' Antony corrected him. In the circumstances it didn't seem altogether tactful to remind his uncle that his going to Chedcombe at all had been the older man's idea, so he substituted a protest. 'You know I hate instant explanations being demanded before I've even had a chance to take breath.'

'Got to admit,' said Vera pacifically, 'what happened will save everyone a lot of bother.'

'With all respect, my dear, I'm not at the moment in a mood to admit anything of the kind. Why a quite simple and orderly defence couldn't be conducted without driving a man well-known in the community to suicide, and thereby creating the kind of scandal I most deplore, I cannot think,' said Sir Nicholas awfully.

'The way it turned out was an accident,' said Antony, without any apology in his tone. He made no attempt to sit down, but put the tea that Jenny now handed to him where his glass of sherry so often stood near the clock. 'You can ask Lisa, I told her exactly what I meant to do, but once both Sandra Linwood and Clifford Elliott turned up at the hotel—'

'You can't tell me you didn't then do your best to bring matters

181

to a head,' said Sir Nicholas. 'However I should like to hear exactly what happened. Had you already come to the conclusion that this man was guilty before you left home?'

'More or less. And in a way it was Sandra herself who brought matters to a head as you call it, though I have to admit I did start the ball rolling.'

Sir Nicholas closed his eyes for a moment as though in pain. 'I know you dislike explanations of any kind,' he said, 'but in view of the interest already displayed by the national press—'

'On Sunday?' asked Antony incredulously.

'Stop press,' said Vera gruffly. 'Sure to have more to say tomorrow though.'

'I was about to remark,' Sir Nicholas went on, 'that I think you owe us an account of what happened.'

'Can't he at least have his tea first,' Jenny protested. She had noticed, as they all had, that her husband was holding himself stiffly as he came in, a sure sign that he was tired and his shoulder painful. Yesterday in all probability he had felt nothing but relief at the way things had turned out; but today the inevitable reaction had set in, and the thing foremost in his mind was Clifford Elliott's untimely death.

Sir Nicholas was in no mood to make allowances. 'He hasn't come from the North Pole,' he pointed out. 'And there's nothing to stop him from drinking his tea while he talks.'

Maitland exchanged a rueful look with his wife and shrugged slightly. 'Better get it over with, love,' he said, and embarked on the required recital, including the reasons he had given to Lisa and Dominic for feeling that he knew the identity of the murderer.

'I imagine you were having a difficult time with Chief Inspector Camden,' said Sir Nicholas with some satisfaction when that part of the narrative was reached. 'Had you realised what this Dr Elliott was going to do?'

'No, of course not. Though I have to admit,' he added honestly, 'that as Vera says it saved an awful lot of bother.'

'Did his letter to the coroner clear everything up?' Vera asked.

'Every last thing. He admitted to having caused Walter Linwood's death, as well as that of the three babies, and to trying to get Henrietta Vaughan blamed. He made a sort of excuse about that, saying he knew she'd be sent for treatment and then released, and fortunately he went into sufficient detail to clear up any doubts the police might otherwise have had.'

'There'll be no need then for the exhumation order to be requested.'

'No, Uncle Nick, and that's the part that's worrying me most. I think he went into so much detail because he was genuinely in love with Sandra, and when he knew how she felt about Walter – she told him clearly enough – he wanted to spare her the pain that digging him up would cause her.'

'Love cannot exactly be taken as an excuse for wholesale murder,' said Sir Nicholas in his most dampening tone. 'Nor is there any need to put the matter quite so colloquially. However,' he added with one of his sudden changes of mood, 'we must be thankful that things are no worse, and at least you'll be spared the necessity of attending the Crown Court at Chedcombe during the Michaelmas Term.'

'Yes, I suppose that is an advantage,' said Maitland warily. 'I spent last night with Lisa and Dominic, and she'll see to all the clearing up there is to be done, and very likely finish up by doing a little match-making between Oliver and Sandra into the bargain. If Dominic doesn't succeed in stopping her, that is.'

'A very capable young lady,' said Sir Nicholas benignly, and exchanged a smile with his wife. It was obvious, Antony thought, that his uncle was unaware of his own and Jenny's knowledge, but it was also quite obvious that Sir Nicholas rather relished the idea of becoming a grandfather, even a never-to-be-acknowledged one, and only by marriage. If only Jenny hadn't been hurt by all this discussion. He turned to look at her, and as though divining his thought she turned to meet his gaze and shook her head.

'We can't go on living in the past,' she said, and there was no doubt about it, her serene look – the look he valued above all others and always thought of by that name – wasn't assumed for his benefit. He'd have seen through that in a moment. 'Now Lisa and that other girl and all the other girls in Chedcombe who are expecting babies will be able to have them without the fear of losing them that way,' she said. 'I think you should be very glad of the way things have turned out, Uncle Nick.'

But that was too much for Sir Nicholas. 'I suppose, since Antony was dealing with the matter, we must be thankful it turned out no worse,' he said repressively. 'But I shudder to think of the kind of sensation the press will make of it.'

'Have a field day,' Vera acknowledged. But she was allowed a latitude with regard to the use of the vernacular that Sir Nicholas denied to his nephew. 'Nothing to worry about though, we'll be out of the country before the end of the week, and Antony and Jenny will be out of town too.'

'That,' said Sir Nicholas, 'is undoubtedly true, and undoubtedly a cause for rejoicing. We may be allowed to live our lives in peace, at least until we come back for the Michaelmas Term.'

And if he had any forebodings about what might be in store for them then he did not voice them, for which unexpected forbearance, as Antony later told Jenny, they must at least be grateful.